LITERARY OUTLAW

A PULP FICTION MAGAZINE | ISSUE #8

IN THIS ISSUE:

SONG OF SILVERGLADE 3
Alistair Foley

MOBY DICK 9
Herman Melville

LEGENDARIUM 19
Michael Bunker
& Kevin G. Summers

FIREHAIR: HEIRESS FOUND 27
John Starr

THE ADVENTURES OF PENROD 37
Booth Tarkington

BLACK CAT: THE BUDDHA'S SECRET 59
Author Unknown

BEREFT 70
Robert Frost

THE WIVES OF THE DEAD 71
Nathaniel Hawthorne

**THE BLACK ORCHIDS
AND THE TALE OF ANNE** 76
Stuart Williams

THE SKULL 83
Philip K. Dick

LITERARY OUTLAW #8
Copyright © 2024 by LiteraryOutlawLLC

Song Of Silverglade | Copyright © 2016 by Alistair Foley
Moby Dick | Public Domain. Originally published in *Thriller Comics Library $157*
Legendarium | Copyright © 2014 by Michael Bunker & Kevin G. Summers
Illustrations by Kent Rockwell | Public Domain.
Firehair: Heiress Found | Public Domain. Originally published in *Ranger Comics #24*
Penrod | Public Domain. Originally published in 1914
Penrod Illustrations by Gordon Hope Grant| Public Domain. Originally published in 1914
Black Cat: The Buddha's Secret | Public Domain. Originally published in *Black Cat #3*
Bereft | Public Domain. Originally published in 1928
The Wives of The Dead | Public Domain. Originally published in 1831
The Black Orchids and the Tale of Anne | Public Domain. Originally published in *Scream #5*
The Skull | Public Domain. Originally published in *If Worlds of Science Fiction, September 1952*

The stories in this magazine are works of fiction. Names, characters, businesses, places, events
and incidents are either the products of the author's imagination or used in a fictitious manner.
Any resemblance to actual persons, living or dead, or actual events is purely coincidental.

All rights reserved. This book or any portion thereof may not be reproduced or used in any
manner whatsoever without the express written permission of the publisher except for the use
of brief quotations in a book review.

www.literaryoutlaw.com

SONG OF SILVERGLADE

BY ALISTAIR FOLEY

1
THE INN OF THE STRUTTING TOM TURKEY

ONCE UPON A TIME, ON A PLANET called Vinworld, a fantasy world that is nothing like the world (most likely Earth) where you are reading this book, there lived a young man named Silverglade. Silverglade was a farm boy who spent his days mucking barn stalls and milking cows and doing all kinds of other work that Americans are too lazy to do. He didn't like his job. Unfortunately, there was nothing he could do about it because Silverglade was very poor and life pretty much sucks for the poor on Earth or Vinworld or anywhere else. Can you dig it?

When I say that Vinworld was nothing like Earth, I don't mean it was completely alien. Like, there were humans and people breathed air and they all spoke in English. And they called a pig and pig and not a moss covered three handled family gredunza. But there were elves and dragons and the like, and people wore renaissance clothes and carried swords and stuff. So, it was kind of like Earth, but the way Earth used to be a long, long time ago in Europe. Also, magic.

Silverglade was so poor because his parents died and left him nothing but an old guitar and an empty bottle of dwarven spirits. He couldn't play the guitar and it was in very bad condition, so he took a job as a farm hand with his mean uncle, who maybe wasn't so mean because he gave Silverglade a job, but he was mean enough that he wouldn't let him practice the guitar. Silverglade really wanted to be a bard, which is about the most useless class you can be in Dungeons & Dragons, but whatever.

So Silverglade spent his days doing farm work and his nights practicing the guitar and writing songs. He wasn't very good at either. When you got right down to it, Silverglade was pretty much only good at shoveling manure, but that is a very useful thing on a farm and it's still classier than certain jobs like politician or lawyer.

Silverglade was shoveling manure one day, cursing his uncle's steed, Mistyofchincoteague, when he heard the rumble of hooves in the distance. Hooves meant more horses, and horses meant more manure, and the farm boy cursed the day he was born.

The horses arrived and on their backs were a bunch of soldiers of the Empire. The Empire was the form of government that the people with all the money and power in that part of Vinworld decided to have that day. They might have chosen to have a republic or whatever, but they chose an empire because reasons. There were about 27 mounted soldiers, each one wearing the black plate mail armor of the Empire. The soldiers climbed down from their horses, kicked the animals for the shear cruelty of it, and then proceeded to march into Silverglade's uncle's house, which was also an inn called, um, The Strutting Tom Turkey.

Poor old Silverglade kept mucking the barn stalls, there were a lot of stalls at the farm, and after that he was going to have to gather and wash the eggs. You might think that eggs come out perfectly clean, but let me tell you, they do not. You've got to wash them, and that was part of Silverglade's job. It was the part he hated the most, even more than shoveling manure, because it made his hands dry and cracked. He had to rub lard all over his hands every night because lotion hadn't been invented yet in Vinworld.

Anyway, Silverglade was down in the hen house, gathering eggs, when he heard a big commotion up at the Inn of the Strutting Tom Turkey. He ran up the hill and looked down at his home, at the only place he had ever lived since his parents died tragically in a golfing accident, and he saw that the inn was burning. A huge plume of black smoke billowed into the air like a plume of smoke from a house fire. Silverglade burst into tears, dropping to his knees dramatically and breaking all of the eggs in his basket.

<insert joke about putting all of your eggs in one basket here>

The Inn of the Strutting Tom Turkey was burning, and Silverglade's guitar was inside. He watched in abject horror as his hopes and dreams went up in smoke. Literally, his dream of being a bard and touring Vinworld was going up in smoke because his guitar was on fire.

The evil soldiers of the Empire were standing around, laughing as they watched the inn burn. They were drinking dwarven spirits right out of the bottle and laughing as Silverglade's uncle screamed inside the burning building.

"That's what you get for not paying your taxes on time," said one of the soldiers cruelly. "Now your inn is on fire and you're dead. Ha Ha Ha."

The other soldiers laughed.

Silverglade did not laugh. He was still crying, thinking about his guitar. Now where was he going to live? How was he going to eat tonight? He thought about eating his uncle's horse, Mistyofchincoteague, but he had no means of curing the meat since all the salt was stored in the house, which was now on fire. You need salt to cure meat, BTW. Most people think meat grows on Styrofoam trays in the back room of the grocery store, but that's not how it works folks. Silverglade watched as the soldiers of the Empire road away. He wished he could think of what to do next, but he couldn't think of anything so he just sat there and waited.

"I'll just sit here and wait," he said dejectedly. "Maybe someone will come along and tell me what to do. If not, I guess I'll just die and the buzzards will pick my bones and poop me out and no one will be around to shovel me into the compost pile."

II
MARKUS THE RED

Silverglade was still sitting on the hillside when a man in red robes approached from the west. He had a cowl pulled low over his eyes and a tall staff with a large, green crystal on the end. Silverglade recognized the stranger at once as Markus the Red, a well-known wizard that came to the Inn of the Strutting Tom Turkey once a year on the Fourth of July to shoot fireworks. They celebrated the Fourth of July in that part of Vinworld because that was the day that something big and important happened in elaborate backstory for this world but I haven't figured out quite yet.

"Hey you," Silverglade said amazedly. "Aren't you Markus the Red?"

"I am Markus the Red," said Markus the Red curiously. "Are you Silverglade, son of Dave."

"I am," said Silverglade precociously. "What are you doing here?"

Markus stared at Silverglade through the shadows of his hood. "I came for you, Silverglade."

"Me?"

"Yes."

"Why?"

"There is an ancient prophecy that the chosen one will someday overthrow the Empire by killing the evil Emperor. You are the chosen one, Silverglade, and someday is today. Or maybe in a couple of days, depending on how many adventures we have between then and now."

"I'm the chosen one?" Silverglade asked in amazement. "How can that be?"

"I have no idea," said Markus amusedly, "that's just how prophecies work. Now come on, saddle up that horse and let's get out of here." Markus stroked his beard, which was also red, knowlingly.

"OK," said Silverglade. "Whatever. There's nothing for me to do around here now anyway." He saddled up Mistyofchincoteague and Silverglade and Markus the Red rode away from the smoldering ruins of the Inn of the Strutting Tom Turkey.

Well, Silverglade rode and Markus jogged. He was on the cross-country team in high school and was a very good runner.

Silverglade stopped as they were about to cross the threshold of the farm's property line. He looked down at Markus, who wasn't even winded yet.

"I'm leaving the place where I lived," Silverglade said somberly, "but it's never really felt like home to me. I don't know if I'll ever come back, so I'd like to take one last look."

He took one last look. The farm looked about the same as it always had, except for the burnt down inn.

"You know," said Silverglade surprisedly, "I don't think I'm going to miss this place at all. Let's get the heck out of here."

III
THE TREASURE OF THE TROLLS

Silverglade and Markus the Red came to clearing in a sylvan wood that everybody on Vinworld said was haunted. No one who had ever entered this forest had come back to tell the tale, but the path

was well maintained enough that Mistyofchincoteague didn't injure her feet on a broken branch or anything like that. The clearing was very scary and there was a big sign on the side of the road that read:

I'D TURN BACK IF I WAS YOU

"Look at that terrible grammar," Markus said annoyedly.

Suddenly, two ugly trolls leapt out of the woods. One had a big beard and was wearing stupid-looking suspenders. The other had a short haircut that stuck up in the front like TinTin.

"My name is Bichael Munker," said the troll with the beard.

"And I'm Cick Nole," said the troll with TinTin hair.

"We're going to kill you and eat you," said Bichael hungrily. "I'll bet you taste good."

"Hahahahahahahahahaha-hahahaha," Cick laughed maniacally and drew a beautiful sword with a jeweled hilt and a glowing blue blade.

Silverglade didn't know what to do since all he had ever done was shovel manure his entire life. He put his arms up to block Cick's blade just as Markus fired a lightning bolt from the end of his staff. Cick fell to the ground like a piece of fried chicken at a Southern Baptist picnic. Bichael charged at Silverglade but was slowed down by the weight of his beard and Silverglade had time to climb down from Mistyofchincoteague and pick up Cick's sword. The blade felt good in his hands. Actually, the hilt felt good because that's the part he was holding. He would get cut real bad if he held the blade because it was so sharp. Silverglade swung the blade as Bichael lunged at him and easily cut the ugly troll in half.

"Wow," Silverglade said unbelievingly, "I'm really good at this swordfighting thing."

"That's because you're the chosen one," said Markus wisely. "It's written that the chosen one will be a natural fighter."

"Where is it written?" Silverglade asked curiously.

"Don't worry about that right now," said Markus smugly. "Hey look at that big pile of armor and weapons over there."

There was a big pile of armor and weapons on the side of the road. It was right next to a big pile of human bones.

"Those must be all the people that came through these woods and never returned," Silverglade lamented.

"Yup," said Markus somberly. "Oh well, you should pick out some stuff so you're ready to fight the Emperor."

"Ok," said Silverglade greedily. He picked out some full plate armor that fit him perfectly. He looked like he could take down an entire army all by himself.

The heroes rode on through the woods and no more monsters bothered them.

IV
THE LEGEND GROWS

Silverglade and Markus had lots of other adventures. They killed 6 dragons, saved a bunch of damsels in distress, found a long lost dwarven mine, defeated an evil wizard named Ason Janspach, and killed a whole bunch of orcs. Their legend grew throughout Vinworld until the Emperor began to worry that this knight called Silverglade might be the chosen one. The Emperor began plotting a way to destroy Silverglade and Markus before Silverglade and Markus could destroy him.

"I know exactly what to do," he said bitterly. "I'll send my entire army to hunt them down and kill them."

V
THE EMPEROR'S ARMY

Silverglade and Markus were having a few beers in a tavern one day when a young woman ran, panting, into the bar.

"There's an army coming into the village," she said affrightedly. "There must be thousands of them." She burst into tears and threw herself into Silverglade's arms. The knight comforted her as he turned to Markus.

"That sounds like the Emperor's Army," he said knowingly.

"Do you think we should fight them or try to get away while we still have time?" Markus asked hesitantly.

"Let's fight them," Silverglade said bravely.

They rushed from the tavern, a spell on Markus's lips and Silverglade drawing his mighty sword. The streets were suddenly filled with five thousand soldiers in black armor. The heroes didn't care, they began cutting into the evil army like a hot knife through butter. Markus took out hundreds at a time with explosive fireballs while Silverglade kept separating bad guy's heads from bad guy's shoulders like an all-star baseball slugger at a whiffleball tournament. After an hour of cutting and explosions the entire army was dead. Then Silverglade and Markus went back into the tavern and order some more beers because they were very thirsty. And then the girl who ran into the tavern, the one who noticed the army, she threw herself at Silverglade and they had a romantic encounter that was very, very steamy.

VI
THE CHOSEN ONE

Silverglade and Markus finished their beers and then decided to head over to the Emperor's castle. They decided to knock on the door and the Emperor's guards decided to open the door.

"Who are you and what do you want?" the guards demanded angrily.

"My name is Silverglade," said Silverglade matter-of-factly, "and this is my sidekick, Markus the Red, and we're here to kill the Emperor. I'm the chosen one."

The guards screamed and threw down their weapons and ran away like a couple of craven cowards. Silverglade and Markus went into the castle and found the Emperor inside. He was sitting on his throne, contemplating his next move.

"What are you doing in my castle?" he demanded hostelry?

"My name is Silverglade," said Silverglade stoically, "and this is my sidekick, Markus the Red, and we're here to kill you because I'm the chosen one."

"Eeeeeeeeeee," screamed the Emperor. He rushed at Silverglade with a magical dagger, but the knight easily deflected the blow and separated the Emperor's head from his shoulders.

"You've done it," Markus cried excitedly. "You killed the Emperor. I knew you could do it."

Silverglade shrugged modestly. "It's all good," he said proudly.

And that's how Silverglade saved the world. He made Markus the new Emperor and went back to the farm where he grew up and hung up his sword over the mantle of the new farmhouse that he built for his new wife, the girl from the tavern in Chapter 5. And they all lived happily ever after, though there were a bunch of other adventures that I'll tell you about some other time.

THE END

Chapter 4. THE GREAT WHITE WHALE

EVERY SHIP THAT PASSED RECEIVED
THE SAME QUESTION FROM AHAB...
AHOY THERE!
HAST THOU SEEN THE
WHITE WHALE? HIM
THEY CALL MOBY DICK—

SOME VESSELS HAD NEWS....
THE SCHOONER "TOWN-HO" FOR
INSTANCE...
AYE! WE
SIGHTED THE BRUTE
NIGH ON TWO YEARS
AGO—OFF TAHITI!
TOWN-HO

THE "BONTON DE ROSE" AND THE "BATCHELOR" HAD SEEN NOTHING—
BUT THE "JERIBOAM" HAD GOOD CAUSE TO REMEMBER MOBY DICK...
AYE, THAT WE HAVE! HE KILLED MY FIRST MATE LAST SPRING — NEAR THE GREAT ICE BARRIER!
JERIBOAM

AFTER THESE VAGUE EXCHANGES OF INFORMATION, AHAB WOULD DASH HIS SPEAKING TRUMPET TO THE DECK AND CRY OUT IN HIS LION-LIKE VOICE —
KEEP HER GOING ROUND THE WORLD! LAY THE TILLER ABACK!

THEY ROUNDED THE CAPE OF GOOD HOPE IN A
TEARING GALE AND STRUCK EASTWARDS TO
THE ORIENT . . .
PERMISSION TO
REEF TOPS'LS,
CAP'N ?
NEVER !
CARRY ON, OR
CARRY UNDER !

THREE MONTHS LATER, "PEQUOD" NEARED JAPANESE WATERS, THOUGHT
BY SOME TO BE THE SUMMER HUNTING GROUND OF THE GREAT WHITE WHALE.
AND IT WAS THERE, TOWARDS SUNSET ONE DAY, THAT ISHMAEL SIGHTED A
WHITE MASS IN THE WATER AHEAD . . .
THE WHITE WHALE !

WITHIN MINUTES, THE THREE WHALEBOATS WERE LOWERED AND TORE TO THE SPOT. AHAB'S BOAT WAS IN ADVANCE ... AND HE SMOTE HIS BROW WITH FURY WHEN HE SAW THE VAST, PULPY MASS AT CLOSE QUARTERS ...
DEMONS TAKE THAT FOOL ISHMAEL— THIS IS NO WHALE!

THE MASS MOVED ... EXTENDED GREAT TENTACLES TO DISCLOSE THE HIDEOUS FORM OF A GIANT WHITE SQUID ...
BACK WATER ALL! FOR THY VERY LIVES — BACK WATER!

A SLIMY COIL AS THICK AS A MAN'S WAIST LAID ITSELF ACROSS THE GUNWHALE ... WITH A FRENZIED CRY, AHAB HACKED AT IT WITH THE BOAT AXE!
AWAY, MONSTER! THOU SHALT NOT HAVE MY BLOOD AND MY BONES ... THEY ARE FOR THE DESTRUCTION OF MOBY DICK!

NOTHING BUT AHAB'S WILD FRENZY COULD HAVE RELEASED THE BOAT FROM THE DOOMED CLUTCHES OF THE GIANT SQUID ... BUT FINALLY THE MONSTER RELAXED ITS HOLD AND SANK IN THE SCARLET-TINGED WATER ...
BACK! BACK TO THE PEQUOD!

TWO DAYS LATER, THEY PASSED CLOSE TO A SHIP MISNAMED THE "DELIGHT", WHICH HAD BUT ONE HALF-SHATTERED WHALEBOAT LEFT...
HAST SEEN THE GREAT WHITE WHALE?
AYE!

THE ANSWER CAME BACK FROM THE TRAGIC-FACED CAPTAIN ON THE QUARTERDECK OF "DELIGHT"...
YESTERDAY! SMASHED TWO BOATS TO MATCHWOOD — CREWS ALL KILLED — DEVIL TAKE MOBY DICK, THE MURDERER!

FROM THAT HOUR FORTH, CAPTAIN AHAB NEVER ATE NOR SLEPT...
CALL ALL HANDS! MAN ALL MASTHEADS! THE FATEFUL HOUR IS AT HAND!

ISHMAEL AND QUEEQUEG KEPT WATCH-AND-WATCH-ABOUT, WITH ANOTHER PAIR AT THE MAIN ROYAL MASTHEAD.
THE TATTOOED HARPOONER SEEMED POSSESSED OF A STRANGE EXCITEMENT. FROM TIME TO TIME HE WOULD TAKE OUT HIS LITTLE EBONY IDOL AND COSSET IT AGAINST HIS BRONZED CHEEK...
AND WHAT DOES YO-JO SAY ABOUT IT ALL, QUEEQUEG?
YO-JO HIM SPEAKEE QUEEQUEG— HIM SAY WE SEE MOBY DICK BYMBYE YOU BET!

YO-JO'S PREDICTION WAS VINDICATED SHORTLY AFTER DAWN THE FOLLOWING DAY...
LOOKEE SEE!

A HUMP LIKE A SNOW-HILL! THREE RAGGED HOLES PUNCHED IN THE STARBOARD FLUKE OF A TWENTY-FOOT TAIL! A DOZEN HARPOONS TWISTED AND WRENCHED AND .TRAILING STREAMERS OF FOUL WEED! THE GREAT WHITE WHALE!

THAR SHE BLOWS!
AND IT'S MOBY DICK!

LEGENDARIUM

BY MICHAEL BUNKER & KEVIN G. SUMMERS

CHAPTER SIX
OR, THE WHALE

THEY APPEARED ON THE HEAVING deck of an old-fashioned sailing ship and knew within seconds into which story they'd arrived. Scrimshaw decorated the gunnels of the ship, and a golden doubloon was nailed to the mainmast. It was a clear, beautiful afternoon at sea, and a man in the crow's-nest high above was bellowing at the top of his lungs.

"There she blows! There she blows! A hump like a snow-hill! It's Moby Dick!"

"I love this story," Bombo and Alistair both said at the exact same moment. The deck rose again as the ship handled the swells, and the two authors looked at each other in amazement. They were both dressed as deck hands from the 1800's, and for the first time since they entered the Legendarium, Alistair's ponytail looked only sort of out of place.

"You *do?*" Bombo asked.

Alistair nodded with a silly grin on his face. "It's my favorite book."

"Five stars?" Bombo said.

"Six. I even have a Moby Dick tattoo. See?" He pulled up the sleeve of his newly acquired sailor shirt to reveal a picture of a white whale's tail and the word *AHAB*.

Bombo shielded his eyes. "TMI, Foley. I really don't want to see that."

He pointed his finger at Alistair. "Two main rules, Foley. No mouth-to-mouth, and we don't show one another our tattoos. Got it?"

The deck of the *Pequod* was a scramble of activity as sailors from all over the ship sprang to life. They clambered into whale boats that were attached to the sides of the big ship and took their places as the smaller boats were lowered toward the ocean. The deep blue sea spread all around them as far as the eye could see, as if the ocean was all there ever was, and all there was ever going to be.

Bombo and Alistair hung back, trying desperately to not get in the way after the disaster with Ernest Hemingway. This was Herman Melville's greatest work, and perhaps the greatest work of American literature. If *Moby Dick* were lost, the repercussions would be catastrophic.

Within minutes, the deck of the *Pequod* was all but empty. Most of the crew was gliding across the water in a desperate race to catch the white whale.

"This is the first day of the chase," Bombo said. "The peak of the novel is on the third day."

"In the last two worlds, the Mome Wraiths attacked near the climax," said Alistair. "Of course, *Moby Dick* isn't like any modern novel. The climax is so spread out… I can't imagine any modern publisher even considering it."

"Yep, it would never happen," Bombo nodded. "And a book where the antagonist is a whale? Not unless the whale was also a robot, or if the whale was anthropomorphized and could communicate to either a young boy or a teenage girl overwrought with angst and brimming with unknown superpowers."

"I agree," Alistair said.

"Melville would probably have to self-publish," said Bombo. "Think about that."

"I'll think about it later," Alistair said. "Right now we've got to figure out how we can save this story."

"You, sailors!" shouted a commanding voice. The writers looked up on the quarterdeck and saw a severe-looking man with a black beard glaring at them. They recognized him at once as Starbuck, the first mate of the *Pequod*. "Get to work, men," he snapped. "I want these decks scrubbed and ready for when they return."

"Yes, sir!" Alistair said.

The writers set themselves to work, formulating their plans as they scrubbed the boards. Bombo lowered a bucket into the ocean and pulled it up again filled with seawater. Meanwhile, Alistair retrieved some soft sandstone, known as holystone, from belowdecks.

"I've been thinking," Alistair said, handing Bombo one of the holystones. "Remember how the doctor in *Beyond the Stars* wanted borogoves, a plant from *Through the Looking Glass?*"

"Yeah."

"And I didn't realize it at the time, but the Cheshire Cat actually suggested to us that we try them. Do you remember that?"

"I think so." Bombo dipped his holystone into the seawater and began to scrub the boards.

"If we had taken some, we would ha've had them when we landed on the space station, and then the captain would have been saved, and the story would have proceeded normally to its original ending."

"The Cat, or the Legendarium, was trying to help us," Bombo said.

"Just like when I found the exact amount of cash that we needed in my wallet," said Alistair. "Anyway, I think it's the revision that caused an opening for the Mome Wraiths to attack." Alistair sank wearily to his knees and began scrubbing. "The Mome Wraiths are like a virus, and the infection starts when the story is allowed to change."

"Same thing happened in *The Pugilist*," Bombo said. "When you decided that you knew better than Ernest Hemingway…"

"I feel like such an idiot," Alistair said.

"I can understand why you would feel that way," said Bombo.

"If I had convinced Agnes to go along with the bet—as appalling as that seems to my modern sensitivity and my sense of moral uprightness—everything would have been different."

Shouts in the distance caught their attention. The writers looked up and saw that the whaling boats had ceased their frantic race across the face of the deep, and sea birds were now circling around the tiny boats.

"Clearly we have to see that *Moby Dick* achieves its original ending."

"Exactly," Alistair said. "We have to watch for any weak point where the Mome Wraiths can attack."

"For all we know, they might already be here," Bombo said. "This novel has a hundred pages about the history of whaling. That was difficult for even *me* to read. If there was any point where they could enter this story, that's it."

"No. The attack is going to come on the third day," Alistair said. "I'm sure of it. Or maybe even in the epilogue. If Ishmael drowns with the rest of the crew, that's it."

"Or if Ahab manages to kill Moby Dick."

"We need to keep our eyes open for any sign of deviation from the original text," said Alistair. "That's our mission. I just wish I'd understood that sooner."

"You're pretty good at analyzing stories," Bombo said. "I hate to pay you a compliment, you being such a blowhard and all, but that really is a strength for you."

"Thanks?"

"I mean it," Bombo said, "I've never outlined a story in my life—"

"No!"

"—or spent five minutes analyzing my stories, but you really have a good understanding of what makes a story work."

"Too bad no one other than slush pile interns have ever read my work," Alistair said.

"That's your own damn fault," said Bombo. "You know what you should do."

"Has anyone ever told you what an annoying jerk you are?" Alistair said.

"My wife tells me that all the time," Bombo said, "and she loves me."

At that moment, in the distance, they both saw the white whale burst from the water like a missile. His jaws were open wide and he was preparing to sink Ahab's boat. The captain prepared to strike with his harpoon, but Moby Dick, showing his malicious intelligence, crashed into the small craft. Ahab was inside the monster's jaws, and Bombo and Alistair stopped their work and stared at the scene unfolding before them. Was this the end?

"Sail on the whale!" screamed Starbuck. "Drive him off!"

Almost instantly, the ship was alive. Starbuck was turning the wheel as sailors pulled at the rigging. Bombo and Alistair dropped their holystones and followed suit, lending their strength to that of the sailors who'd remained on board when the whaling boats lowered. As he pulled, Bombo realized that he was standing right behind Ishmael, the omniscient protagonist of the novel.

The *Pequod* raced across the waves as Ahab slipped from the jaws of death and into the sea. Moby Dick swam around the bobbing sailors like a shark, but the ship effectively parted the whale from his victims and drove him off.

The captain and his men were hauled back on board the *Pequod*, and the old man was raving all the while about the condition of his harpoon and the eternal sap of vengeance that was coursing in his veins. Having been the first to spot the white whale, Ahab claimed the doubloon that was nailed to the mainmast.

Night closed around the *Pequod* as Ahab ordered the ship to keep full before the wind. They did not want to overrun the white whale in the night.

Bombo and Alistair found their bunks belowdecks and waited anxiously for morning. And throughout the long night, the old man paced back and forth on deck, his false leg tap-tap-tapping on the boards overhead.

★ ★ ★

THEY WERE UP AT DAYBREAK ON THE SEC-
ond day. The sailors rose without complaint and set about their business as the
Pequod plowed through the sea, leaving
great, foamy furrows in her wake. As the
men went about their duties, Alistair
worked and thought on what was supposed to happen today. They would spot
Moby Dick a second time, and once
again mad Captain Ahab would lower
after the white whale. The rest Alistair
knew by heart as well. Once again Ahab's

ship would be capsized, and this time the
enigmatic harpooner Fedallah would be
lost at sea.

The masthead cry came as if on cue.
"There she blows! She blows—right
ahead!"

The crew of the *Pequod* moved as
one man as Moby Dick breached. The
men scrambled toward their boats, ready
to slay the monster upon whose head
Ahab had bent his fury.

"Breach your last to the sun, Moby
Dick," said the old man, "thy hour and
thy harpoon are at hand."

The boats were lowered, but Moby Dick did not flee as he had done before. He turned toward the tiny boats and met them head-on. He was intent on annihilating every plank of these mortals who pursued him. The whale was pierced all over with rusted harpoons, and now, as Bombo and Alistair got their first close look at the monster, they saw something peculiar.

"Do you see that?" Bombo said. "Sticking right there, near the whale's dorsal fin?"

Alistair looked closer, and his eyes widened when he saw it. There was a sword plunged halfway into Moby Dick's back.

"Is that the vorpal sword?" Alistair asked. "It looks just like the same sword Commander Stuyvesant was using back on the *Alamo-02*."

"I think so," said Bombo.

"You know what that means!" Alistair said. "We need to be on one of the whaling boats tomorrow. To end this endless procession of stories in peril, we need to retrieve that sword."

"That's all you," said Bombo, shaking his head. "I really, really don't like water."

"Fine," Alistair said. "I'll do it."

At that moment, Ahab heaved his spear at Moby Dick. It sank into the whale, and as the line tightened, Fedallah, Ahab's harpooner, was pulled from the boat.

The whale darted, and the lines extending from his flanks dragged two boats across the water. They smashed together, sending a dozen or more sailors into the sea. Ahab cut his line as the white whale turned and smashed his boat.

The whale departed, allowing Ahab one final opportunity to turn from his vain attempt at vengeance. Once again, the captain was dragged back on board the *Pequod*, and everyone took it as an ill omen when they saw that his ivory leg had been shattered.

"Sir," said Starbuck, "Shall we keep chasing this murderous fish till he swamps the last man? Shall we be dragged by him to the bottom of the sea?"

Ahab had a pensive look upon his face. His harpooner was dead and his false leg shattered, all because of his quest for vengeance on a dumb beast. "Perhaps you're right," he said. "Might be we should abandon this chase and return to Nantucket. We've lost so much already."

Every shadow on the *Pequod* seemed to be alive, to almost strain with expectation. Alistair and Bombo knew immediately that this was it, the moment when the story could change and, in the process, be wiped from existence. Knowing the consequences if they allowed that to happen, Alistair and Bombo both sprang into action.

"No!" Bombo shouted. He stepped forward and raised his hand like a senator in ancient Rome, rising to speak before Caesar. "He took your leg and the Parsee's life," he shouted. "No! You *must* kill the white whale."

"A dead whale or a stove boat," shouted Alistair. "You *must* slay Moby Dick!"

Ahab's features hardened as he turned his back on Starbuck. "Ahab is forever Ahab, men. I am the Fates' lieutenant. Aye, men, Moby Dick will rise once more, but only to spout his last."

In the hours that followed, a new leg was fashioned for the captain, and the sails were shortened as on the previous night. Ishmael was chosen to replace Fedallah on Ahab's boat, just as it had happened in the novel. The next day would be the last, either for Ahab or for this world.

★ ★ ★

THE MORNING OF THE THIRD DAY dawned fair and fresh, but this time Moby Dick was nowhere to be seen.

"We've sailed over him," Ahab said. "Aye, he's chasing *me* now, not I him." He ordered the ship turned into the wind, to the dismay of Starbuck.

An hour went by before the mad captain saw his prey. When he did, he spoke in a long soliloquy that was at the same time poetic, unrealistic, and utterly insane. It was brilliant writing—touching and frightening. Even two such diverse tastes as Bombo Dawson and Alistair Foley could agree on that, and they couldn't find much at all on which they could agree.

"It's time," Alistair said. He moved closer so that only Bombo could hear him. "Don't forget that after the whale destroys Ahab's boat, Moby Dick is going to ram the *Pequod* and destroy the ship. You're going to need to find something to hang on to."

"I'll stick like glue to that coffin," Bombo said, indicating the wooden box built for the harpooner Queequeg earlier in the novel. After the cannibal had recovered from his illness, the coffin had been turned into a life buoy.

"To the boats!" Ahab cried.

Alistair and Bombo moved toward Ahab's boat, and only then did they realize the flaw in their plan. Only one member of Ahab's crew had been lost the previous day, and Ishmael, the novel's protagonist, was meant to replace that man in the captain's boat. There was only the one available spot in the boat, and if Alistair took it, Ishmael would be killed on the *Pequod* when the ship went down.

Ishmael couldn't die. He was telling the story. He needed to live.

Bombo and Alistair looked at each other, each searching the other's face for an answer. *What are we going to do?* they thought.

A thought crossed Bombo's mind, and he didn't give it much time to linger at all. He acted immediately. Stepping up behind another member of Ahab's crew, the large man tapped the crewman on the shoulder. When the sailor turned around, Bombo dropped him with a single punch to the jaw.

"That's for Ernest Hemingway," Bombo said.

Alistair climbed onto the boat behind Ishmael and they lowered into the sea. Sharks circled around them, biting at their oars as they pulled with everything they had. Then the white whale breached, and the men saw, to their horror, the body of Fedallah bound to Moby Dick's flanks by a spider web of ropes.

"Pull on!" Ahab ordered. The ship came alongside the whale as Moby Dick turned to face them once more. His horrible teeth reminded Alistair of the Cheshire Cat, and the teacher recalled what would happen should he fail once more in the quest to recover the vorpal sword. He couldn't let that happen.

"Towards thee I roll," Ahab said, "thou all-destroying but unconquering whale. To the last I grapple with thee; from hell's heart I stab at thee; for hate's sake I spit my last breath at thee. Sink all coffins and all hearses to one common pool, and since neither can be mine, let me then tow to pieces while still chasing thee, though tied to thee, thou damned whale! Thus I give up the spear!"

The captain threw his harpoon as Moby Dick surged forward. Alistair stood up in the boat, waited for just the right moment, and then leapt upon the white whale. His hands closed over the hilt of the vorpal sword. At that same moment, Ahab's own line caught the captain around the neck and he was pulled from the boat.

Back on the *Pequod*, Bombo watched the scene unfolding before him. Ahab was in the water, being towed behind Moby Dick as the whale smashed up the other boats. Alistair clung to the monster's back, screaming in terror as he held onto the vorpal sword for dear life. The white whale charged in malicious fury toward the *Pequod* and rammed her with all the force of hatred that had existed in the world since it was made.

Bombo held fast to the coffin life buoy as it hit the water. He took a deep breath and held it as he sank beneath the surface and the waves rolled over his head.

THE DRAMA'S DONE. WHY THEN HERE does anyone step forth? Because *three* did survive the wreck.

The coffin, lovingly built by the carpenter's hand, bobbed to the surface at the heart of a great swirling eddy. Bombo held fast to the life buoy, his beard frizzing out in a thousand directions as he coughed and stammered for breath. He first came upon Ishmael, the lone survivor of the original novel, and pulled the brooding man on board their peculiar craft. There was no sign of Alistair. For long moments it was as if the sound had been turned down, or perhaps the air had been sucked out of the universe. Bombo began to wonder if they had failed in their mission, and he thought that maybe Mome Wraiths would soon be circling the survivors like the sharks. But

there were no living shadows in the sky, and though the sea was alive with sharks, no Mome Wraiths could be seen.

"There!" Ishmael cried. He pointed to a dark spot in the water.

Bombo reached into the deep and plucked out his greatest critic with one hairy hand. Alistair was soaked to the bone, but he held in his hand the vorpal sword that they had so long sought.

"What do you think of Melville now?" Bombo asked.

"*Seven* stars," Alistair gasped. He spewed out sea water and then smiled at Bombo. "Best. Novel. Ever."

Bombo smiled back. "What now? Do we wait for the *Rachel?*"

"The *Rachel?*" asked Ishmael. "The ship we met a few days back that was searching for her lost crewmen?"

"She's going to find you tomorrow," Alistair said. "Just hang on and you'll be rescued."

"How do you know this?" asked Ishmael.

"He's read the book," Bombo said. "I mean, um… do you have any donuts?"

"I think there's another way out of here," said Alistair.

Bombo looked around at the limitless expanse of ocean, stretching beyond the horizon. "Oh?"

"Let's open the coffin."

They slid into the water as the sharks circled closer and closer. Bombo ran his fingers across the opening and pushed open the lid of the coffin. White light poured through.

"You first," Bombo said. He helped Alistair to climb inside, then followed after him a second later.

TO BE CONCLUDED IN LITERARY OUTLAW #9

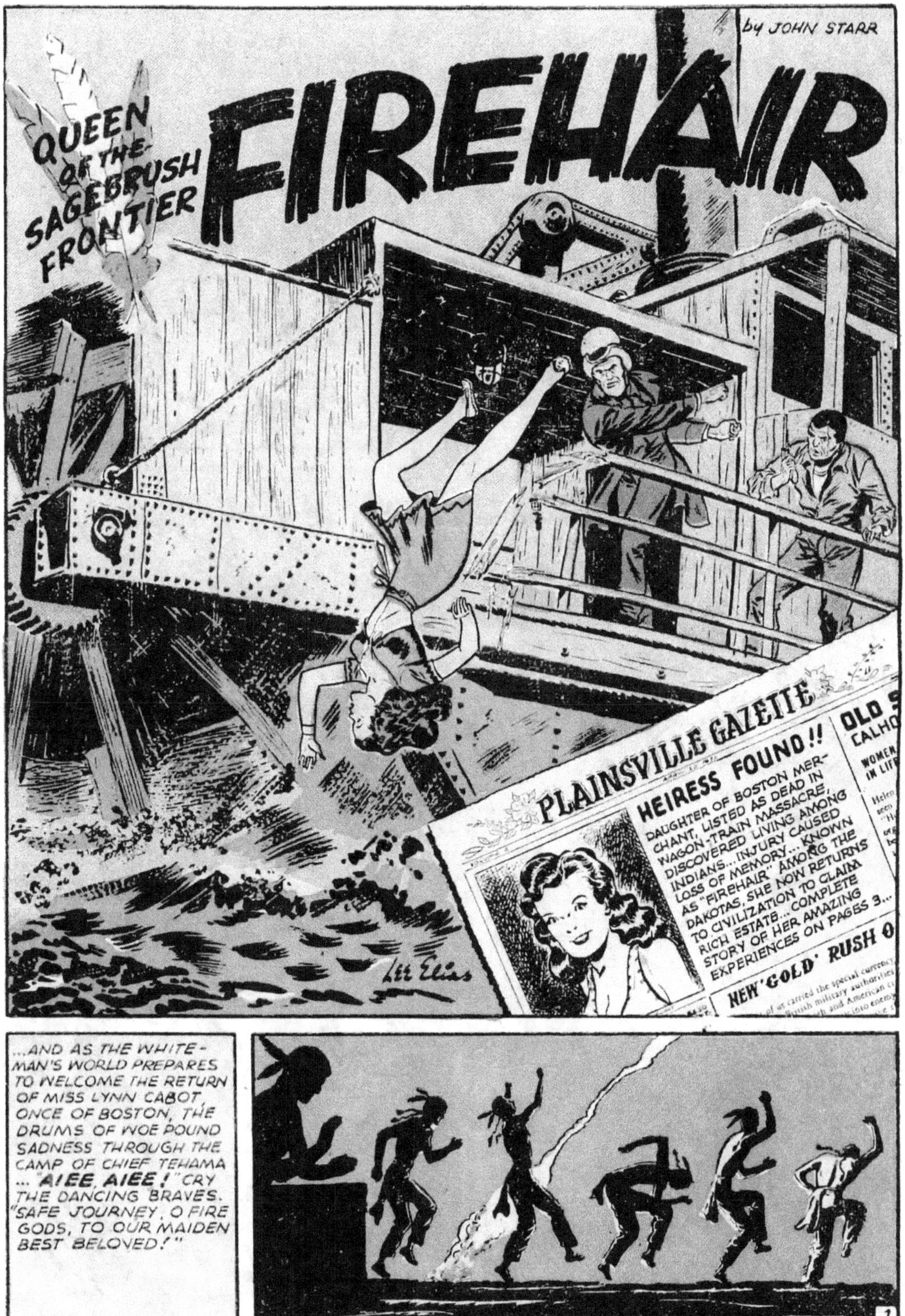

...AND AS THE WHITE-MAN'S WORLD PREPARES TO WELCOME THE RETURN OF MISS LYNN CABOT, ONCE OF BOSTON, THE DRUMS OF WOE POUND SADNESS THROUGH THE CAMP OF CHIEF TEHAMA ... *"AIEE, AIEE!"* CRY THE DANCING BRAVES. "SAFE JOURNEY, O FIRE GODS, TO OUR MAIDEN BEST BELOVED!"

COME, DAUGHTER, THE HORSES WAIT... HAVE YOU SPOKEN YOUR FAREWELLS?
AYE, O TEHAMA, AND MY HEART WEEPS.

TO LITTLE AX AND TO YOU I OWE MY LIFE. I SHALL NEVER FORGET...
NOR SHALL WE FIREHAIR, WHAT IS IT MY SON?
THE SMALL ONES FATHER.

HIM NAME WAMPUM... HIM WATCH FIREHAIR'S NEW TEEPEE.
BEADS STRONG MEDICINE TO PROTECT YOU.
OH, THANK YOU. THANK YOU!

I MUST NOT LET THEM SEE MY TEARS... HOW MUCH I DREAD TO GO!

BUT YOU MUST GO, PRINCESS! YOU ARE JOHN CABOT'S DAUGHTER...
I KNOW, FATHER... I KNOW!

And SOON...
FAREWELL FIREHAIR! BUT OUR HEARTS RIDE WITH YOU WHEREVER YOU RIDE!
2

AND MILES BEYOND, WHERE A PACKET BOAT CHURNS THE RIVER, HER WHITE BRETHREN PREPARE TO WELCOME THE LONG-LOST FIREHAIR...

BUT I STILL DON'T SAVVY THE DEAL, LUKE. WHAT'S OUR PITCH WITH THIS RED-HEAD SQUAW?
YEAH... SHE COMES ABOARD TOMORROW, AN' THEN WHAT, LUKE?
AN' THEN WE FIX HER LITTLE WAGON, THAT'S WHAT!

PRESCOTT HISSELF FIGGERED THIS STUNT, AN' YO'RE TH' KEY TO IT, SAL...LISSEN-

NEXT DAY... THE WHITE MAN'S LANDING LIES BELOW- WE GO NO FARTHER, FIREHAIR.
THEN FAREWELL, TEHAMA-FAREWELL MY BROTHER, LITTLE AX!

AND YOU, MY OWN BLAZE- BE PATIENT UNTIL I SEND FOR YOU!

TURN YOUR HORSE, MY SON. THEN FOLLOW HER SECRETLY, AS I BADE, AND SEE NO HARM BEFALLS HER!
YOUR WORD IS MY WILL, O FATHER!

SOON...
LOOK YONDER, SAL—THERE WITH HER BUNDLE!
YOU MEAN I'M SUPPOSED TO LOOK LIKE THAT—THAT SCARECROW!

WHEN WE RED YORE TOPKNOT AN' DRESS YOU UP, WHOSE GONNA TELL TH' DIFF'RENCE?
WELL, I HOPE JIM PRESCOTT KNOWS WHAT HE'S DOIN'.

THAT NIGHT, ON DECK...
HERE'S HER CABIN... JUST KNOCK AN' SPILL THE GAB I TOLD YOU!
OKAY— HERE GOES!

WHAT IS IT, WAMPUM? OH— SOMEBODY AT THE DOOR!

YOU SAVVY TRADE, TALK GIRL? MY FATHER HEAP SICKUM— YOU COME HELPUM?

WHY OF COURSE I'LL HELP! WHICH CABIN? OH, WHAT'S THIS?
GRAB 'ER, SCAR, AN' HUSH HER YAP— QUICK!

YEE-OW! SHE BIT MY HAND! CAN'T HOLD 'ER NO MORE'N A PANTHER!
JUMP 'ER, LUKE— SHE'S GETTIN' LOOSE— OOOF!

CLAWS LIKE A CAT! GIT HER OFF ME— THE RAIL!
THIS'LL FIX HER!

RAIL BUSTED— KNOCKED 'ER PLUMB OVER!
CLAW ME, WILL SHE!
HELP— HELP!

I'LL BLAST HER TO HELL—
NO, YOU FOOL— PADDLE-WHEEL GOT HER! BEAT IT!

BUT IN THE PACKET'S FOAMING WAKE—
FIRE-STICK TALK— SQUAW YELP— LITTLE AX HURRY!

AND THIS IS WHAT THE MOON-LIGHT SAW, SECONDS LATER...

LATER... MY HEAD_ BETTER NOW... BUT IF YOUR FATHER HAD NOT SENT YOU AFTER ME_
OUR GODS STOOD ON WATCH FOR YOU, SISTER...COME_I MAKE FIRE!

ATTACKED BY STRANGERS AND I KNOW NOT WHY... HOW CAN WE OVERTAKE THE WHEEL-BOAT?
WHITE MAN'S VILLAGE THAT WAY... MAYBE HORSES THERE...WE GO SEE.

BEHOLD! I CUT THEM LOOSE_
WE ARE NOT THIEVES, LITTLE AX...I SHALL BUY THEM_WAIT.

INSIDE THE SALOON...
NOSSIR, I DON'T DRINK, SMOKE NOR GAMBLE. I_
H_HEY_ LOOK!
WHISKEY 25¢

GENTLEMEN, I'M BUYING TWO OF THE HORSES AT THE HITCHRACK
NOT MINE YOU AIN'T!

THIS PISTOL SAYS I AM! HERE'S MY I.O.U. FOR A THOUSAND DOLLARS, COLLECTABLE AT PLAINS-VILLE...IF YOU'D RATHER BE PAID IN BULLETS_ TRY TO STOP ME!
REWARD

YONDER SHE GOES, CHUCK. DO WE ROUSE TH' BOYS AN' TAKE AFTER 'EM?
UNUNH_NOT HARDLY...ANY GAL WHO SHOOTS THAT QUICK, HER I.O.U IS GOOD WITH ME!

MEANWHILE, AT PLAINS-VILLE...
TAKE 'ER EASY, SAL... PRESCOTT'LL STEER YUH THROUGH TH' REST.
I AIN'T SCARED... IT'S THESE DEER-SKINS ITCH ME!

IS THAT HER - THE HEIRESS?
HUMPH! LOOKS LIKE A HUSSY TO ME!
WHEE-EW! I'D TAKE 'ER WITHOUT HER MILLION DOLLARS!
WHO'S THAT TAKIN' HER ARM?
IT'S JIM PRESCOTT... HE'S HAND-LIN' HER ESTATE FER TH' BOSTON BANKERS.
BEST LAWYER IN TH' STATE, PRESCOTT IS... HE'D MAKE US A FINE GOV'NOR!

STEP IN, MISS CABOT... THE LEGAL PAPERS ARE BEING CHECKED... THEY'LL BE READY FOR YOU THIS EVENING.

PSSST! HOW'S IT GOIN', JIM?
IT'S IN THE BAG... THREE MORE HOURS AND WE'RE ON EASY STREET!

BUT AT THE EDGE OF TOWN.
BOAT STILL AT THE DOCK... WE MADE IT IN TIME!

FEED THESE HORSES WELL, BOY... WE ARE WITNESSES FOR THE INDIAN HEIRESS... WHERE IS SHE?
STOCKMEN'S HOTEL... THE WHOLE TOWN'S THERE FOR A LOOK AT 'ER.

HAH! DRESSED IN MY CLOTHES... IT IS AS I SUS-PECTED!
BUT WHAT CAN WE DO? WHO WILL HELP US?
HOTEL

AS DARKNESS FALLS...
WE MUST HELP OURSELVES, MY BROTHER...HERE, THIS MESSAGE FOR THE SHERIFF!
YOU RISK TOO MUCH FIREHAIR... BUT I GO!
THIS GIRL OF THE BOAT WHO POSES AS FIREHAIR...THEIR DEVIL-TRY WAS DEEPLY PLANNED, BUT IF I CAN GET MY HANDS ON HER- AAH.
HER WINDOW! AND NOW, IF THE NIGHT GODS ARE KIND-
INSIDE...
I AIN'T NO CHAMBER-MAID! WHY DO I GOTTA WASH THIS WOLF-PUP?
BECAUSE HE SMELLS- AN' HE'S GOT FLEAS, TOO- AN' I GOT TO CARRY HIM!
AN' LOOKIT THIS! I'M CIVILIZED, BALDY, AN' THIS STUFF ITCHES ...FIVE HUNDRED EASY DOLLARS, HUH? WHY I-
THE WINDOW- LOOK!
THE SQUAW GIRL- AND ALIVE!
JUMPIN' SNAKES- MY PISTOL!

HO! HERE IS MEDICINE FOR YOUR SICK FATHER, SNAKE-TONGUE!

AND FOR YOU— MY FINGERS AT YOUR THROAT!
SHE'S CRAZY— SHE'LL KILL ME. HELP!

NO, I WON'T KILL YOU... I NEED YOU ALIVE TO TALK!

NOW, IMPOSTOR— BEGIN! I WANT TO KNOW—
THE DOOR— SOMEBODY COMING!

C'MON— WE'RE ALL SET BELOW— HEY! BALDY—WHAT?
STEADY! ONE MOVE, ONE SOUND, AND YOU'RE DEAD!

MINUTES LATER...
SO THE JUDGE IS IN THE PARLOR— PAPERS READY TO SIGN? HOW NICE!
D-DON'T. DON'T SHOOT! I'LL CONFESS IT ALL, LADY.

VERY WISE TO NAME YOU ADMINISTRATOR OF THE ESTATE, MR. PRESCOTT.
YES, TOO MUCH MONEY FOR A YOUNG GIRL TO HANDLE... AH- HERE THEY COME!
BUT THAT ISN'T- IT'S THE WRONG GIRL!
SHE'S WISE, BOSS! OUR DEAL IS SUNK!
YOU, LAWYER, DROP THAT GUN!
I AM JOHN CABOT'S DAUGHTER AND I WANT WHAT'S MINE... DROP THAT GUN, I SAID - HAA!
MY WRIST! SCAR-LUKE JUMP HER, YOU FOOLS!
HOLD IT, GENTS! THE LAW'S TAKIN' OVER FROM HERE!
LATER...
I-I ONLY DONE WHAT LUKE TOLD ME!
I'M AN INNOCENT GIRL...LUKE SWORE IT WAS ONLY A JOKE!
PRESCOTT- HE HIRED ME-
IT'S A FRAME-UP, A PACK OF LIES! I DEMAND A FAIR TRIAL!
WAL, THEY'RE LOCKED UP NOW!
PUT 'EM WHERE YA WANT 'EM, PARDNER- I'LL DRAW 'EM!
YES, MISS CABOT, NOW REAL JUSTICE CAN BE SERVED- THANKS TO YOU!

THE ADVENTURES OF PENROD

BY BOOTH TARKINGTON

CHAPTER XXIV
LITTLE
GENTLEMAN

THE MIDSUMMER SUN WAS STINGING hot outside the little barber-shop next to the corner drug store and Penrod, undergoing a toilette preliminary to his very slowly approaching twelfth birthday, was adhesive enough to retain upon his face much hair as it fell from the shears. There is a mystery here: the tonsorial processes are not unagreeable to manhood; in truth, they are soothing; but the hairs detached from a boy's head get into his eyes, his ears, his nose, his mouth, and down his neck, and he does everywhere itch excruciatingly. Wherefore he blinks, winks, weeps, twitches, condenses his countenance, and squirms; and perchance the barber's scissors clip more than intended—belike an outlying flange of ear.

"Um—muh—OW!" said Penrod, this thing having happened.

"D' I touch y' up a little?" inquired the barber, smiling falsely.

"Ooh—UH!" The boy in the chair offered inarticulate protest, as the wound was rubbed with alum.

"THAT don't hurt!" said the barber. "You WILL get it, though, if you don't sit stiller," he continued, nipping in the bud any attempt on the part of his patient to think that he already had "it."

"Pfuff!" said Penrod, meaning no disrespect, but endeavoring to dislodge a temporary moustache from his lip.

"You ought to see how still that little Georgie Bassett sits," the barber went on, reprovingly. "I hear everybody says he's the best boy in town."

"Pfuff! PHIRR!" There was a touch of intentional contempt in this.

"I haven't heard nobody around the neighbourhood makin' no such remarks," added the barber, "about nobody of the name of Penrod Schofield."

"Well," said Penrod, clearing his mouth after a struggle, "who wants 'em to? Ouch!"

"I hear they call Georgie Bassett the 'little gentleman,'" ventured the barber, provocatively, meeting with instant success.

"They better not call ME that," returned Penrod truculently. "I'd like to hear anybody try. Just once, that's all! I bet they'd never try it ag—OUCH!"

"Why? What'd you do to 'em?"

"It's all right what I'd DO! I bet they wouldn't want to call me that again long as they lived!"

"What'd you do if it was a little girl? You wouldn't hit her, would you?"

"Well, I'd—Ouch!"

"You wouldn't hit a little girl, would you?" the barber persisted, gathering into his powerful fingers a mop of hair from the top of Penrod's head and pulling that suffering head into an unnatural position. "Doesn't the Bible say it ain't never right to hit the weak sex?"

"Ow! SAY, look OUT!"

"So you'd go and punch a pore, weak, little girl, would you?" said the barber, reprovingly.

"Well, who said I'd hit her?" demanded the chivalrous Penrod. "I bet I'd FIX her though, all right. She'd see!"

"You wouldn't call her names, would you?"

"No, I wouldn't! What hurt is it to call anybody names?"

"Is that SO!" exclaimed the barber. "Then you was intending what I heard you hollering at Fisher's grocery delivery wagon driver fer a favour, the other day when I was goin' by your house, was you? I reckon I better tell him, because he says to me after-WERDS if he ever lays eyes on you when you ain't in your own yard, he's goin' to do a whole lot o' things you ain't goin' to like! Yessir, that's what he says to ME!"

"He better catch me first, I guess, before he talks so much."

"Well," resumed the barber, "that ain't sayin' what you'd do if a young lady ever walked up and called you a little gentleman. *I* want to hear what you'd do to her. I guess I know, though—come to think of it."

"What?" demanded Penrod.

"You'd sick that pore ole dog of yours on her cat, if she had one, I expect," guessed the barber derisively.

"No, I would not!"

"Well, what WOULD you do?"

"I'd do enough. Don't worry about that!"

"Well, suppose it was a boy, then: what'd you do if a boy come up to you and says, 'Hello, little gentleman'?"

"He'd be lucky," said Penrod, with a sinister frown, "if he got home alive."

"Suppose it was a boy twice your size?"

"Just let him try," said Penrod ominously. "You just let him try. He'd never see daylight again; that's all!"

The barber dug ten active fingers into the helpless scalp before him and did his best to displace it, while the anguished Penrod, becoming instantly a seething crucible of emotion, misdirected his natural resentment into maddened brooding upon what he would do to a boy "twice his size" who should dare to call him "little gentleman." The barber shook him as his father had never shaken him; the barber buffeted him, rocked him frantically to and fro; the barber seemed to be trying to wring his neck; and Penrod saw himself in staggering zigzag pictures, destroying large, screaming, fragmentary boys who had insulted him.

The torture stopped suddenly; and clenched, weeping eyes began to see again, while the barber applied cooling lotions which made Penrod smell like a coloured housemaid's ideal.

"Now what," asked the barber, combing the reeking locks gently, "what would it make you so mad fer, to have somebody call you a little gentleman? It's a kind of compliment, as it were, you might say. What would you want to hit anybody fer THAT fer?"

To the mind of Penrod, this question was without meaning or reasonableness. It was within neither his power nor his desire to analyze the process by which the phrase had become offensive to him, and was now rapidly assuming

the proportions of an outrage. He knew only that his gorge rose at the thought of it.

"You just let 'em try it!" he said threateningly, as he slid down from the chair. And as he went out of the door, after further conversation on the same subject, he called back those warning words once more: "Just let 'em try it! Just once—that's all *I* ask 'em to. They'll find out what they GET!"

The barber chuckled. Then a fly lit on the barber's nose and he slapped at it, and the slap missed the fly but did not miss the nose. The barber was irritated. At this moment his birdlike eye gleamed a gleam as it fell upon customers approaching: the prettiest little girl in the world, leading by the hand her baby brother, Mitchy-Mitch, coming to have Mitchy-Mitch's hair clipped, against the heat.

It was a hot day and idle, with little to feed the mind—and the barber was a mischievous man with an irritated nose. He did his worst.

Meanwhile, the brooding Penrod pursued his homeward way; no great distance, but long enough for several one-sided conflicts with malign insulters made of thin air. "You better NOT call me that!" he muttered. "You just try it, and you'll get what other people got when THEY tried it. You better not ack fresh with ME! Oh, you WILL, will you?" He delivered a vicious kick full upon the shins of an iron fence-post, which suffered little, though Penrod instantly regretted his indiscretion. "Oof!" he grunted, hopping; and went on after bestowing a look of awful hostility upon the fence-post. "I guess you'll know better next time," he said, in parting, to this antagonist. "You just let me catch you around here again and

I'll—" His voice sank to inarticulate but ominous murmurings. He was in a dangerous mood.

Nearing home, however, his belligerent spirit was diverted to happier interests by the discovery that some workmen had left a caldron of tar in the cross-street, close by his father's stable. He tested it, but found it inedible. Also, as a substitute for professional chewing-gum it was unsatisfactory, being insufficiently boiled down and too thin, though of a pleasant, lukewarm temperature. But it had an excess of one quality—it was sticky. It was the stickiest tar Penrod had ever used for any purposes whatsoever, and nothing upon which he wiped his hands served to rid them of it; neither his polka-dotted shirt waist nor his knickerbockers; neither the fence, nor even Duke, who came unthinkingly wagging out to greet him, and retired wiser.

Nevertheless, tar is tar. Much can be done with it, no matter what its condition; so Penrod lingered by the caldron, though from a neighbouring yard could be heard the voices of comrades, including that of Sam Williams. On the ground about the caldron were scattered chips and sticks and bits of wood to the number of a great multitude. Penrod mixed quantities of this refuse into the tar, and interested himself in seeing how much of it he could keep moving in slow swirls upon the ebon surface.

Other surprises were arranged for the absent workmen. The caldron was almost full, and the surface of the tar near the rim.

Penrod endeavoured to ascertain how many pebbles and brickbats, dropped in, would cause an overflow. Labouring heartily to this end, he had almost accomplished it, when he received the suggestion for an experiment on a much larger scale. Embedded at the corner of a grassplot across the street was a whitewashed stone, the size of a small watermelon and serving no purpose whatever save the questionable one of decoration. It was easily pried up with a stick; though getting it to the caldron tested the full strength of the ardent labourer. Instructed to perform such a task, he would have sincerely maintained its impossibility but now, as it was unbidden, and promised rather destructive results, he set about it with unconquerable energy, feeling certain that he would be rewarded with a mighty splash. Perspiring, grunting vehemently, his back aching and all muscles strained, he progressed in short stages until the big stone lay at the base of the caldron. He rested a moment, panting, then lifted the stone, and was bending his shoulders for the heave that would lift it over the rim, when a sweet, taunting voice, close behind him, startled him cruelly.

"How do you do, LITTLE GENTLEMAN!"

Penrod squawked, dropped the stone, and shouted, "Shut up, you dern fool!" purely from instinct, even before his about-face made him aware who had so spitefully addressed him.

It was Marjorie Jones. Always dainty, and prettily dressed, she was in speckless and starchy white to-day, and a refreshing picture she made, with the new-shorn and powerfully scented Mitchy-Mitch clinging to her hand. They had stolen up behind the toiler, and now stood laughing together in sweet merriment. Since the passing of Penrod's Rupe Collins period he had experienced some severe qualms at the recollection of his last meeting with

Marjorie and his Apache behaviour; in truth, his heart instantly became as wax at sight of her, and he would have offered her fair speech; but, alas! in Marjorie's wonderful eyes there shone a consciousness of new powers for his undoing, and she denied him opportunity.

"Oh, OH!" she cried, mocking his pained outcry. "What a way for a LITTLE GENTLEMAN to talk! Little gentleman don't say wicked—"

"Marjorie!" Penrod, enraged and dismayed, felt himself stung beyond all endurance. Insult from her was bitterer to endure than from any other. "Don't you call me that again!"

"Why not, LITTLE GENTLE-MAN?"

He stamped his foot. "You better stop!"

Marjorie sent into his furious face her lovely, spiteful laughter.

"Little gentleman, little gentleman, little gentleman!" she said deliberately. "How's the little gentleman, this afternoon? Hello, little gentleman!"

Penrod, quite beside himself, danced eccentrically. "Dry up!" he howled. "Dry up, dry up, dry up, dry UP!"

Mitchy-Mitch shouted with delight and applied a finger to the side of the caldron—a finger immediately snatched away and wiped upon a handkerchief by his fastidious sister.

"'Ittle gellamun!" said Mitchy-Mitch.

"You better look out!" Penrod whirled upon this small offender with grim satisfaction. Here was at least something male that could without dishonour be held responsible. "You say that again, and I'll give you the worst—"

"You will NOT!" snapped Marjorie, instantly vitriolic. "He'll say just whatever he wants to, and he'll say it just as MUCH as he wants to. Say it again, Mitchy-Mitch!"

"'Ittle gellamun!" said Mitchy-Mitch promptly.

"Ow-YAH!" Penrod's tone-production was becoming affected by his mental condition. "You say that again, and I'll—"

"Go on, Mitchy-Mitch," cried Marjorie. "He can't do a thing. He don't DARE! Say it some more, Mitchy-Mitch—say it a whole lot!"

Mitchy-Mitch, his small, fat face shining with confidence in his immunity, complied.

"'Ittle gellamun!" he squeaked malevolently. ",Ittle gellamun! ,Ittle gellamun! ,Ittle gellamun!"

The desperate Penrod bent over the whitewashed rock, lifted it, and then—outdoing Porthos, John Ridd, and Ursus in one miraculous burst of strength—heaved it into the air.

Marjorie screamed.

But it was too late. The big stone descended into the precise midst of the caldron and Penrod got his mighty splash. It was far, far beyond his expectations.

Spontaneously there were grand and awful effects—volcanic spectacles of nightmare and eruption. A black sheet of eccentric shape rose out of the caldron and descended upon the three children, who had no time to evade it.

After it fell, Mitchy-Mitch, who stood nearest the caldron, was the thickest, though there was enough for all. Br'er Rabbit would have fled from any of them.

CHAPTER XXV
TAR

WHEN MARJORIE AND MITCHY-Mitch got their breath, they used it vocally; and seldom have more penetrating sounds issued from human throats. Coincidentally, Marjorie, quite baresark, laid hands upon the largest stick within reach and fell upon Penrod with blind fury. He had the presence of mind to flee, and they went round and round the caldron, while Mitchy-Mitch feebly endeavoured to follow—his appearance, in this pursuit, being pathetically like that of a bug fished out of an ink-well, alive but discouraged.

Attracted by the riot, Samuel Williams made his appearance, vaulting a fence, and was immediately followed by Maurice Levy and Georgie Bassett. They stared incredulously at the extraordinary spectacle before them.

"Little GEN-TIL-MUN!" shrieked Marjorie, with a wild stroke that landed full upon Penrod's tarry cap.

"OOOCH!" bleated Penrod.

"It's Penrod!" shouted Sam Williams, recognizing him by the voice. For an instant he had been in some doubt.

"Penrod Schofield!" exclaimed Georgie Bassett. "WHAT does this mean?" That was Georgie's style, and had helped to win him his title.

Marjorie leaned, panting, upon her stick. "I cu-called—uh—him—oh!" she sobbed—"I called him a lul-little—oh—gentleman! And oh—lul-look!—oh! lul-look at my du-dress! Lul-look at Mumitchy—oh—Mitch—oh!"

Unexpectedly, she smote again—with results—and then, seizing the indistinguishable hand of Mitchy-Mitch, she ran wailing homeward down the street.

"'Little gentleman'?" said Georgie Bassett, with some evidences of disturbed complacency. "Why, that's what they call ME!"

"Yes, and you ARE one, too!" shouted the maddened Penrod. "But you better not let anybody call ME that! I've stood enough around here for one day, and you can't run over ME, Georgie Bassett. Just you put that in your gizzard and smoke it!"

"Anybody has a perfect right," said Georgie, with, dignity, "to call a person a little gentleman. There's lots of names nobody ought to call, but this one's a NICE—"

"You better look out!"

Unavenged bruises were distributed all over Penrod, both upon his body and upon his spirit. Driven by subtle forces, he had dipped his hands in catastrophe and disaster: it was not for a Georgie Bassett to beard him. Penrod was about to run amuck.

"I haven't called you a little gentleman, yet," said Georgie. "I only said it. Anybody's got a right to SAY it."

"Not around ME! You just try it again and—"

"I shall say it," returned Georgie, "all I please. Anybody in this town has a right to SAY 'little gentleman'—"

Bellowing insanely, Penrod plunged his right hand into the caldron, rushed upon Georgie and made awful work of his hair and features.

Alas, it was but the beginning! Sam Williams and Maurice Levy screamed with delight, and, simultaneously infected, danced about the struggling pair, shouting frantically:

"Little gentleman! Little gentleman! Sick him, Georgie! Sick him, little gentleman! Little gentleman! Little gentleman!"

The infuriated outlaw turned upon them with blows and more tar, which gave Georgie Bassett his opportunity and later seriously impaired the purity of his fame. Feeling himself hopelessly tarred, he dipped both hands repeatedly into the caldron and applied his gatherings to Penrod. It was bringing coals to Newcastle, but it helped to assuage the just wrath of Georgie.

The four boys gave a fine imitation of the Laocoon group complicated by an extra figure frantic splutterings and chokings, strange cries and stranger words issued from this tangle; hands dipped lavishly into the inexhaustible reservoir of tar, with more and more picturesque results. The caldron had been elevated upon bricks and was not perfectly balanced; and under a heavy impact of the struggling group it lurched and went partly over, pouring forth a Stygian tide which formed a deep pool in the gutter.

It was the fate of Master Roderick Bitts, that exclusive and immaculate person, to make his appearance upon the chaotic scene at this juncture. All in the cool of a white "sailor suit," he turned aside from the path of duty—which led straight to the house of a maiden aunt—and paused to hop with joy upon the sidewalk. A repeated epithet continuously half panted, half squawked, somewhere in the nest of gladiators, caught his ear, and he took it up excitedly, not knowing why.

"Little gentleman!" shouted Roderick, jumping up and down in childish glee. "Little gentleman! Little gentleman! Lit—"

A frightful figure tore itself free from the group, encircled this innocent bystander with a black arm, and hurled him headlong. Full length and flat on his face went Roderick into the Stygian pool. The frightful figure was Penrod.

Instantly, the pack flung themselves upon him again, and, carrying them with him, he went over upon Roderick, who from that instant was as active a belligerent as any there.

Thus began the Great Tar Fight, the origin of which proved, afterward, so difficult for parents to trace, owing to the opposing accounts of the combatants. Marjorie said Penrod began it; Penrod said Mitchy-Mitch began it; Sam Williams said Georgie Bassett began it; Georgie and Maurice Levy said Penrod began it; Roderick Bitts, who had not recognized his first assailant, said Sam Williams began it.

Nobody thought of accusing the barber. But the barber did not begin it; it was the fly on the barber's nose that began it—though, of course, something else began the fly. Somehow, we never manage to hang the real offender.

The end came only with the arrival of Penrod's mother, who had been having a painful conversation by telephone with Mrs. Jones, the mother of Marjorie, and came forth to seek an errant son. It is a mystery how she was able to pick out her own, for by the time she got there his voice was too hoarse to be recognizable. Mr. Schofield's version of things was that Penrod was insane. "He's a stark, raving lunatic!" declared the father, descending to the library from a before-dinner interview with the outlaw, that evening. "I'd send him to military school, but I don't believe they'd take him. Do you know WHY he says all that awfulness happened?"

"When Margaret and I were trying to scrub him," responded Mrs.

Schofield wearily, "he said 'everybody' had been calling him names."

"‚Names!'" snorted her husband. "'Little gentleman!' THAT'S the vile epithet they called him! And because of it he wrecks the peace of six homes!"

"SH! Yes; he told us about it," said Mrs. Schofield, moaning. "He told us several hundred times, I should guess, though I didn't count. He's got it fixed in his head, and we couldn't get it out. All we could do was to put him in the closet. He'd have gone out again after those boys if we hadn't. I don't know WHAT to make of him!"

"He's a mystery to ME!" said her husband. "And he refuses to explain why he objects to being called 'little gentleman.' Says he'd do the same thing—and worse—if anybody dared to call him that again. He said if the President of the United States called him that he'd try to whip him. How long did you have him locked up in the closet?"

"SH!" said Mrs. Schofield warningly. "About two hours; but I don't think it softened his spirit at all, because when I took him to the barber's to get his hair clipped again, on account of the tar in it, Sammy Williams and Maurice Levy were there for the same reason, and they just WHISPERED 'little gentleman,' so low you could hardly hear them—and Penrod began fighting with them right before me, and it was really all the barber and I could do to drag him away from them. The barber was very kind about it, but Penrod—"

"I tell you he's a lunatic!" Mr. Schofield would have said the same thing of a Frenchman infuriated by the epithet "camel." The philosophy of insult needs expounding.

"SH!" said Mrs. Schofield. "It does seem a kind of frenzy."

"Why on earth should any sane person mind being called—"

"SH!" said Mrs. Schofield. "It's beyond ME!"

"What are you SH-ing me for?" demanded Mr. Schofield explosively.

"SH!" said Mrs. Schofield. "It's Mr. Kinosling, the new rector of Saint Joseph's."

"Where?"

"SH! On the front porch with Margaret; he's going to stay for dinner. I do hope—"

"Bachelor, isn't he?"

"Yes."

"OUR old minister was speaking of him the other day," said Mr. Schofield, "and he didn't seem so terribly impressed."

"SH! Yes; about thirty, and of course so superior to most of Margaret's friends—boys home from college. She thinks she likes young Robert Williams, I know—but he laughs so much! Of course there isn't any comparison. Mr. Kinosling talks so intellectually; it's a good thing for Margaret to hear that kind of thing, for a change and, of course, he's very spiritual. He seems very much interested in her." She paused to muse. "I think Margaret likes him; he's so different, too. It's the third time he's dropped in this week, and I—"

"Well," said Mr. Schofield grimly, "if you and Margaret want him to come again, you'd better not let him see Penrod."

"But he's asked to see him; he seems interested in meeting all the family. And Penrod nearly always behaves fairly well at table." She paused, and then put to her husband a question referring to his interview with Penrod upstairs. "Did you—did you—do it?"

"No," he answered gloomily. "No, I didn't, but—" He was interrupted by a violent crash of china and metal in the kitchen, a shriek from Della, and the outrageous voice of Penrod. The well-informed Della, ill-inspired to set up for a wit, had ventured to address the scion of the house roguishly as "little gentleman," and Penrod, by means of the rapid elevation of his right foot, had removed from her supporting hands a laden tray. Both parents, started for the kitchen, Mr. Schofield completing his interrupted sentence on the way.

"But I will, now!"

The rite thus promised was hastily but accurately performed in that apartment most distant from the front porch; and, twenty minutes later, Penrod descended to dinner. The Rev. Mr. Kinosling had asked for the pleasure of meeting him, and it had been decided that the only course possible was to cover up the scandal for the present, and to offer an undisturbed and smiling family surface to the gaze of the visitor.

Scorched but not bowed, the smouldering Penrod was led forward for the social formulae simultaneously with the somewhat bleak departure of Robert Williams, who took his guitar with him, this time, and went in forlorn unconsciousness of the powerful forces already set in secret motion to be his allies.

The punishment just undergone had but made the haughty and unyielding soul of Penrod more stalwart in revolt; he was unconquered. Every time the one intolerable insult had been offered him, his resentment had become the hotter, his vengeance the more instant and furious. And, still burning with outrage, but upheld by the conviction of right, he was determined to continue to the last drop of his blood the defense of his honour, whenever it should be assailed, no matter how mighty or august the powers that attacked it. In all ways, he was a very sore boy.

During the brief ceremony of presentation, his usually inscrutable countenance wore an expression interpreted by his father as one of insane obstinacy, while Mrs. Schofield found it an incentive to inward prayer. The fine graciousness of Mr. Kinosling, however, was unimpaired by the glare of virulent suspicion given him by this little brother: Mr. Kinosling mistook it for a natural curiosity concerning one who might possibly become, in time, a member of the family. He patted Penrod upon the head, which was, for many reasons, in no condition to be patted with any pleasure to the patter. Penrod felt himself in the presence of a new enemy.

"How do you do, my little lad," said Mr. Kinosling. "I trust we shall become fast friends."

To the ear of his little lad, it seemed he said, "A trost we shall bick-home fawst frainds." Mr. Kinosling's pronunciation was, in fact, slightly precious; and, the little lad, simply mistaking it for some cryptic form of mockery of himself, assumed a manner and expression which argued so ill for the proposed friendship that Mrs. Schofield hastily interposed the suggestion of dinner, and the small procession went in to the dining-room.

"It has been a delicious day," said Mr. Kinosling, presently; "warm but balmy." With a benevolent smile he addressed Penrod, who sat opposite him. "I suppose, little gentleman, you have been indulging in the usual outdoor sports of vacation?"

Penrod laid down his fork and glared, open-mouthed at Mr. Kinosling.

"You'll have another slice of breast of the chicken?" Mr. Schofield inquired, loudly and quickly.

"A lovely day!" exclaimed Margaret, with equal promptitude and emphasis. "Lovely, oh, lovely! Lovely!"

"Beautiful, beautiful, beautiful!" said Mrs. Schofield, and after a glance at Penrod which confirmed her impression that he intended to say something, she continued, "Yes, beautiful, beautiful, beautiful, beautiful, beautiful beautiful!"

Penrod closed his mouth and sank back in his chair—and his relatives took breath.

Mr. Kinosling looked pleased. This responsive family, with its ready enthusiasm, made the kind of audience he liked. He passed a delicate white hand gracefully over his tall, pale forehead, and smiled indulgently.

"Youth relaxes in summer," he said. "Boyhood is the age of relaxation; one is playful, light, free, unfettered. One runs and leaps and enjoys one's self with one's companions. It is good for the little lads to play with their friends; they jostle, push, and wrestle, and simulate little, happy struggles with one another in harmless conflict. The young muscles are toughening. It is good. Boyish chivalry develops, enlarges, expands. The young learn quickly, intuitively, spontaneously. They perceive the obligations of noblesse oblige. They begin to comprehend the necessity of caste and its requirements. They learn what birth means—ah,—that is, they learn what it means to be well born. They learn courtesy in their games; they learn politeness, consideration for one another in their pastimes, amusements, lighter occupations. I make it my pleasure to join them often, for I sympathize with them in all their wholesome joys as well as in their little bothers and perplexities. I understand them, you see; and let me tell you it is no easy matter to understand the little lads and lassies." He sent to each listener his beaming glance, and, permitting it to come to rest upon Penrod, inquired:

"And what do you say to that, little gentleman?"

Mr. Schofield uttered a stentorian cough. "More? You'd better have some more chicken! More! Do!"

"More chicken!" urged Margaret simultaneously. "Do please! Please! More! Do! More!"

"Beautiful, beautiful," began Mrs. Schofield. "Beautiful, beautiful, beautiful, beautiful—"

It is not known in what light Mr. Kinosling viewed the expression of Penrod's face. Perhaps he mistook it for awe; perhaps he received no impression at all of its extraordinary quality. He was a rather self-engrossed young man, just then engaged in a double occupation, for he not only talked, but supplied from his own consciousness a critical though favourable auditor as well, which of course kept him quite busy. Besides, it is oftener than is expected the case that extremely peculiar expressions upon the countenances of boys are entirely overlooked, and suggest nothing to the minds of people staring straight at them. Certainly Penrod's expression—which, to the perception of his family, was perfectly horrible—caused not the faintest perturbation in the breast of Mr. Kinosling.

Mr. Kinosling waived the chicken, and continued to talk. "Yes, I think I may claim to understand boys," he said, smiling thoughtfully. "One has been a boy one's self. Ah, it is not all playtime! I hope our young scholar here does not overwork himself at his Latin, at his classics, as I did, so that at the age of eight years I was compelled to wear glasses. He must be careful not to strain the little eyes at his scholar's tasks, not to let the little shoulders grow round over his scholar's desk. Youth is golden;

we should keep it golden, bright, glistening. Youth should frolic, should be sprightly; it should play its cricket, its tennis, its hand-ball. It should run and leap; it should laugh, should sing madrigals and glees, carol with the lark, ring out in chanties, folk-songs, ballads, roundelays—"

He talked on. At any instant Mr. Schofield held himself ready to cough vehemently and shout, "More chicken," to drown out Penrod in case the fatal words again fell from those eloquent lips; and Mrs. Schofield and Margaret kept themselves prepared at all times to assist him. So passed a threatening meal, which Mrs. Schofield hurried, by every means with decency, to its conclusion. She felt that somehow they would all be safer out in the dark of the front porch, and led the way thither as soon as possible.

"No cigar, I thank you." Mr. Kinosling, establishing himself in a wicker chair beside Margaret, waved away her father's proffer. "I do not smoke. I have never tasted tobacco in any form." Mrs. Schofield was confirmed in her opinion that this would be an ideal son-in-law. Mr. Schofield was not so sure.

"No," said Mr. Kinosling. "No tobacco for me. No cigar, no pipe, no cigarette, no cheroot. For me, a book—a volume of poems, perhaps. Verses, rhymes, lines metrical and cadenced—those are my dissipation. Tennyson by preference: 'Maud,' or 'Idylls of the King'—poetry of the sound Victorian days; there is none later. Or Longfellow will rest me in a tired hour. Yes; for me, a book, a volume in the hand, held lightly between the fingers."

Mr. Kinosling looked pleasantly at his fingers as he spoke, waving his hand in a curving gesture which brought it into the light of a window faintly illumined from the interior of the house. Then he passed those graceful fingers over his hair, and turned toward Penrod, who was perched upon the railing in a dark corner.

"The evening is touched with a slight coolness," said Mr. Kinosling. "Perhaps I may request the little gentleman—"

"B'gr-r-RUFF!" coughed Mr. Schofield. "You'd better change your mind about a cigar."

"No, I thank you. I was about to request the lit—"

"DO try one," Margaret urged. "I'm sure papa's are nice ones. Do try—"

"No, I thank you. I remarked a slight coolness in the air, and my hat is in the hallway. I was about to request—"

"I'll get it for you," said Penrod suddenly.

"If you will be so good," said Mr. Kinosling. "It is a black bowler hat, little gentleman, and placed upon a table in the hall."

"I know where it is." Penrod entered the door, and a feeling of relief, mutually experienced, carried from one to another of his three relatives their interchanged congratulations that he had recovered his sanity.

"'The day is done, and the darkness,'" began Mr. Kinosling—and recited that poem entire. He followed it with "The Children's Hour," and after a pause, at the close, to allow his listeners time for a little reflection upon his rendition, he passed his hand again over his head, and called, in the direction of the doorway:

"I believe I will take my hat now, little gentleman."

"Here it is," said Penrod, unexpectedly climbing over the porch railing, in the other direction. His mother and father and Margaret had supposed him to be standing in the hallway out of deference, and because he thought it tactful not to interrupt the recitations. All of them remembered, later, that this supposed thoughtfulness on his part struck them as unnatural.

"Very good, little gentleman!" said Mr. Kinosling, and being somewhat chilled, placed the hat firmly upon his head, pulling it down as far as it would go. It had a pleasant warmth, which he noticed at once. The next instant, he noticed something else, a peculiar sensation of the scalp—a sensation which he was quite unable to define. He lifted his hand to take the hat off, and entered upon a strange experience: his hat seemed to have decided to remain where it was.

"Do you like Tennyson as much as Longfellow, Mr. Kinosling?" inquired Margaret.

"I—ah—I cannot say," he returned absently. "I—ah—each has his own—ugh! flavour and savour, each his—ah—ah—"

Struck by a strangeness in his tone, she peered at him curiously through the dusk. His outlines were indistinct, but she made out that his arms were, uplifted in a singular gesture. He seemed to be wrenching at his head.

"Is—is anything the matter?" she asked anxiously. "Mr. Kinosling, are you ill?"

"Not at—ugh!—all," he replied, in the same odd tone. "I—ah—I believe—UGH!"

He dropped his hands from his hat, and rose. His manner was slightly agitated. "I fear I may have taken a trifling—ah—cold. I should—ah—perhaps be—ah—better at home. I will—ah—say good-night."

At the steps, he instinctively lifted his hand to remove his hat, but did not do so, and, saying "Goodnight," again in a frigid voice, departed with visible stiffness from that house, to return no more.

"Well, of all—!" cried Mrs. Schofield, astounded. "What was the matter? He just went—like that!" She made a flurried gesture. "In heaven's name, Margaret, what DID you say to him?"

"*I!*" exclaimed Margaret indignantly. "Nothing! He just WENT!"

"Why, he didn't even take off his hat when he said good-night!" said Mrs. Schofield.

Margaret, who had crossed to the doorway, caught the ghost of a whisper behind her, where stood Penrod.

"YOU BET HE DIDN'T!"

He knew not that he was overheard.

A frightful suspicion flashed through Margaret's mind—a suspicion that Mr. Kinosling's hat would have to be either boiled off or shaved off. With growing horror she recalled Penrod's long absence when he went to bring the hat.

"Penrod," she cried, "let me see your hands!"

She had toiled at those hands herself late that afternoon, nearly scalding her own, but at last achieving a lily purity.

"Let me see your hands!"

She seized them.

Again they were tarred!

CHAPTER XXVI
THE QUIET AFTERNOON

Perhaps middle-aged people might discern Nature's real intentions in the matter of pain if they would examine a boy's punishments and sorrows, for he prolongs neither beyond their actual duration. With a boy, trouble must be of Homeric dimensions to last over-night. To him, every next day is really a new day. Thus, Penrod woke, next morning, with neither the unspared rod, nor Mr. Kinosling in his mind. Tar, itself, so far as his consideration of it went, might have been an undiscovered substance. His mood was cheerful and mercantile; some process having worked mysteriously within him, during the night, to the result that his first waking thought was of profits connected with the sale of old iron—or perhaps a ragman had passed the house, just before he woke.

By ten o'clock he had formed a partnership with the indeed amiable Sam, and the firm of Schofield and Williams plunged headlong into commerce. Heavy dealings in rags, paper, old iron and lead gave the firm a balance of twenty-two cents on the evening of the third day; but a venture in glassware, following, proved disappointing on account of the scepticism of all the druggists in that part of town, even after seven laborious hours had been spent in cleansing a wheelbarrow-load of old medicine bottles with hydrant water and ashes. Likewise, the partners were disheartened by their failure to dispose of a crop of "greens," although they had uprooted specimens of that decorative and unappreciated flower, the dandelion, with such persistence and energy that the Schofields' and Williams' lawns looked curiously haggard for the rest of that summer.

The fit passed: business languished; became extinct. The dog-days had set in.

One August afternoon was so hot that even boys sought indoor shade. In the dimness of the vacant carriage-house of the stable, lounged Masters Penrod Schofield, Samuel Williams, Maurice Levy, Georgie Bassett, and Herman. They sat still and talked. It is a hot day, in rare truth, when boys devote themselves principally to conversation, and this day was that hot.

Their elders should beware such days. Peril hovers near when the fierceness of weather forces inaction and boys in groups are quiet. The more closely volcanoes, Western rivers, nitroglycerin, and boys are pent, the deadlier is their action at the point of outbreak. Thus, parents and guardians should look for outrages of the most singular violence and of the most peculiar nature during the confining weather of February and August.

The thing which befell upon this broiling afternoon began to brew and stew peacefully enough. All was innocence and languor; no one could have foretold the eruption.

They were upon their great theme: "When I get to be a man!" Being human, though boys, they considered their present estate too commonplace to be dwelt upon. So, when the old men gather, they say: "When I was a boy!" It really is the land of nowadays that we never discover.

"When I'm a man," said Sam Williams, "I'm goin' to hire me a couple of coloured waiters to swing me in a hammock and keep pourin' ice-water on me all day out o' those waterin'-cans they sprinkle flowers from. I'll hire you for one of 'em, Herman."

"No; you ain' goin' to," said Herman promptly. "You ain' no flowuh. But nev' min' nat, anyway. Ain' nobody goin' haih me whens *I'm* a man. Goin' be my own boss. *I'm* go' be a rai'road man!"

"You mean like a superintendent, or sumpthing like that, and sell tickets?" asked Penrod.

"Sup'in—nev' min' nat! Sell ticket? NO suh! Go' be a PO'tuh! My uncle a po'tuh right now. Solid gole buttons—oh, oh!"

"Generals get a lot more buttons than porters," said Penrod. "Generals—"

"Po'tuhs make the bes' l'vin'," Herman interrupted. "My uncle spen' mo' money 'n any white man n'is town."

"Well, I rather be a general," said Penrod, "or a senator, or sumpthing like that."

"Senators live in Warshington," Maurice Levy contributed the information. "I been there. Warshington ain't so much; Niag'ra Falls is a hundred times as good as Warshington. So's 'Tlantic City, I was there, too. I been everywhere there is. I—"

"Well, anyway," said Sam Williams, raising his voice in order to obtain the floor, "anyway, I'm goin' to lay in a hammock all day, and have ice-water sprinkled on top o' me, and I'm goin' to lay there all night, too, and the next day. I'm goin' to lay there a couple o' years, maybe."

"I bet you don't!" exclaimed Maurice. "What'd you do in winter?"

"What?"

"What you goin' to do when it's winter, out in a hammock with water

sprinkled on top o' you all day? I bet you—"

"I'd stay right there," Sam declared, with strong conviction, blinking as he looked out through the open doors at the dazzling lawn and trees, trembling in the heat. "They couldn't sprinkle too much for ME!"

"It'd make icicles all over you, and—"

"I wish it would," said Sam. "I'd eat 'em up."

"And it'd snow on you—"

"Yay! I'd swaller it as fast as it'd come down. I wish I had a BARREL o' snow right now. I wish this whole barn was full of it. I wish they wasn't anything in the whole world except just good ole snow."

Penrod and Herman rose and went out to the hydrant, where they drank long and ardently. Sam was still talking about snow when they returned.

"No, I wouldn't just roll in it. I'd stick it all round inside my clo'es, and fill my hat. No, I'd freeze a big pile of it all hard, and I'd roll her out flat and then I'd carry her down to some ole tailor's and have him make me a SUIT out of her, and—"

"Can't you keep still about your ole snow?" demanded Penrod petulantly. "Makes me so thirsty I can't keep still, and I've drunk so much now I bet I bust. That ole hydrant water's mighty near hot anyway."

"I'm goin' to have a big store, when I grow up," volunteered Maurice.

"Candy store?" asked Penrod.

"NO, sir! I'll have candy in it, but not to eat, so much. It's goin' to be a deportment store: ladies' clothes, gentlemen's clothes, neckties, china goods, leather goods, nice lines in woollings and lace goods—"

"Yay! I wouldn't give a five-for-a-cent marble for your whole store," said Sam. "Would you, Penrod?"

"Not for ten of 'em; not for a million of 'em! *I'm* goin' to have—"

"Wait!" clamoured Maurice. "You'd be foolish, because they'd be a toy deportment in my store where they'd be a hunderd marbles! So, how much would you think your five-for-a-cent marble counts for? And when I'm keepin' my store I'm goin' to get married."

"Yay!" shrieked Sam derisively. "MARRIED! Listen!" Penrod and Herman joined in the howl of contempt.

"Certumly I'll get married," asserted Maurice stoutly. "I'll get married to Marjorie Jones. She likes me awful good, and I'm her beau."

"What makes you think so?" inquired Penrod in a cryptic voice.

"Because she's my beau, too," came the prompt answer. "I'm her beau because she's my beau; I guess that's plenty reason! I'll get married to her as soon as I get my store running nice."

Penrod looked upon him darkly, but, for the moment, held his peace.

"Married!" jeered Sam Williams. "Married to Marjorie Jones! You're the only boy I ever heard say he was going to get married. I wouldn't get married for—why, I wouldn't for—for—" Unable to think of any inducement the mere mention of which would not be ridiculously incommensurate, he proceeded: "I wouldn't do it! What you want to get married for? What do married people do, except just come home tired, and worry around and kind of scold? You better not do it, M'rice; you'll be mighty sorry."

"Everybody gets married," stated Maurice, holding his ground.

"They gotta."

"I'll bet *I* don't!" Sam returned hotly. "They better catch me before they tell ME I have to. Anyway, I bet nobody has to get married unless they want to."

"They do, too," insisted Maurice. "They GOTTA!"

"Who told you?"

"Look at what my own papa told me!" cried Maurice, heated with argument. "Didn't he tell me your papa had to marry your mamma, or else he never'd got to handle a cent of her money? Certumly, people gotta marry. Everybody. You don't know anybody over twenty years old that isn't married—except maybe teachers."

"Look at policemen!" shouted Sam triumphantly. "You don't s'pose anybody can make policemen get married, I reckon, do you?"

"Well, policemen, maybe," Maurice was forced to admit. "Policemen and teachers don't, but everybody else gotta."

"Well, I'll be a policeman," said Sam. "THEN I guess they won't come around tellin' me I have to get married. What you goin' to be, Penrod?"

"Chief police," said the laconic Penrod.

"What you?" Sam inquired of quiet Georgie Bassett.

"I am going to be," said Georgie, consciously, "a minister."

This announcement created a sensation so profound that it was followed by silence. Herman was the first to speak.

"You mean preachuh?" he asked incredulously. "You go' PREACH?"

"Yes," answered Georgie, looking like Saint Cecilia at the organ.

Herman was impressed. "You know all 'at preachuh talk?"

"I'm going to learn it," said Georgie simply.

"How loud kin you holler?" asked Herman doubtfully.

"He can't holler at all," Penrod interposed with scorn. "He hollers like a girl. He's the poorest hollerer in town!"

Herman shook his head. Evidently he thought Georgie's chance of being ordained very slender. Nevertheless, a final question put to the candidate by the coloured expert seemed to admit one ray of hope.

"How good kin you clim a pole?"

"He can't climb one at all," Penrod answered for Georgie. "Over at Sam's turning-pole you ought to see him try to—"

"Preachers don't have to climb poles," Georgie said with dignity.

"GOOD ones do," declared Herman. "Bes' one ev' *I* hear, he clim up an' down same as a circus man. One n'em big 'vivals outen whens we livin' on a fahm, preachuh clim big pole right in a middle o' the church, what was to hol' roof up. He clim way high up, an' holler: 'Goin' to heavum, goin' to heavum, goin' to heavum NOW. Hallelujah, praise my Lawd!' An' he slide down little, an' holler: 'Devil's got a hol' o' my coat-tails; devil tryin' to drag me down! Sinnuhs, take wawnun! Devil got a hol' o' my coat-tails; I'm a-goin' to hell, oh Lawd!' Nex', he clim up little mo', an' yell an' holler: 'Done shuck ole devil loose; goin' straight to heavum agin! Goin' to heavum, goin' to heavum, my Lawd!' Nex', he slide down some mo' an' holler, 'Leggo my coat-tails, ole devil! Goin' to hell agin, sinnuhs! Goin' straight to hell, my Lawd!' An' he clim an' he slide, an' he slide, an' he clim, an' all time holler: 'Now 'm a-goin' to heavum; now 'm a-goin' to

hell! Goin'to heavum, heavum, heavum, my Lawd!' Las' he slide all a-way down, jes' a-squallin' an' a-kickin' an' a-rarin' up an' squealin', 'Goin' to hell. Goin' to hell! Ole Satum got my soul! Goin' to hell! Goin' to hell! Goin' to hell, hell, hell!'"

Herman possessed that extraordinary facility for vivid acting which is the great native gift of his race, and he enchained his listeners. They sat fascinated and spellbound.

"Herman, tell that again!" said Penrod, breathlessly.

Herman, nothing loath, accepted the encore and repeated the Miltonic episode, expanding it somewhat, and dwelling with a fine art upon those portions of the narrative which he perceived to be most exciting to his audience. Plainly, they thrilled less to Paradise gained than to its losing, and the dreadful climax of the descent into the Pit was the greatest treat of all.

The effect was immense and instant. Penrod sprang to his feet.

"Georgie Bassett couldn't do that to save his life," he declared. "*I'm* goin' to be a preacher! I'D be all right for one, wouldn't I, Herman?"

"So am I!" Sam Williams echoed loudly. "I guess I can do it if YOU can. I'd be better'n Penrod, wouldn't I, Herman?"

"I am, too!" Maurice shouted. "I got a stronger voice than anybody here, and I'd like to know what—"

The three clamoured together indistinguishably, each asserting his qualifications for the ministry according to Herman's theory, which had been accepted by these sudden converts without question.

"Listen to ME!" Maurice bellowed, proving his claim to at least the voice by drowning the others. "Maybe I can't climb a pole so good, but who can holler louder'n this? Listen to ME-E-E!"

"Shut up!" cried Penrod, irritated. "Go to heaven; go to hell!"

"Oo-o-oh!" exclaimed Georgie Bassett, profoundly shocked.

Sam and Maurice, awed by Penrod's daring, ceased from turmoil, staring wide-eyed.

"You cursed and swore!" said Georgie.

"I did not!" cried Penrod, hotly. "That isn't swearing."

"You said, 'Go to a big H'!" said Georgie.

"I did not! I said, 'Go to heaven,' before I said a big H. That isn't swearing, is it, Herman? It's almost what the preacher said, ain't it, Herman? It ain't swearing now, any more—not if you put 'go to heaven' with it, is it, Herman? You can say it all you want to, long as you say 'go to heaven' first, CAN'T you, Herman? Anybody can say it if the preacher says it, can't they, Herman? I guess I know when I ain't swearing, don't I, Herman?"

Judge Herman ruled for the defendant, and Penrod was considered to have carried his point. With fine consistency, the conclave established that it was proper for the general public to "say it," provided "go to heaven" should in all cases precede it. This prefix was pronounced a perfect disinfectant, removing all odour of impiety or insult; and, with the exception of Georgie Bassett (who maintained that the minister's words were "going" and "gone," not "go"), all the boys proceeded to exercise their new privilege so lavishly that they tired of it.

But there was no diminution of evangelical ardour; again were heard the clamours of dispute as to which was the best qualified for the ministry, each of the claimants appealing passionately to Herman, who, pleased but confused, appeared to be incapable of arriving at a decision.

During a pause, Georgie Bassett asserted his prior rights. "Who said it first, I'd like to know?" he demanded. "I was going to be a minister from long back of to-day, I guess. And I guess I said I was going to be a minister right to-day before any of you said anything at all. DIDN'T I, Herman? YOU heard me, didn't you, Herman? That's the very thing started you talking about it, wasn't it, Herman?"

"You' right," said Herman. "You the firs' one to say it."

Penrod, Sam, and Maurice immediately lost faith in Herman.

"What if you did say it first?" Penrod shouted. "You couldn't BE a minister if you were a hunderd years old!"

"I bet his mother wouldn't let him be one," said Sam. "She never lets him do anything."

"She would, too," retorted Georgie. "Ever since I was little, she—"

"He's too sissy to be a preacher!" cried Maurice. "Listen at his squeaky voice!"

"I'm going to be a better minister," shouted Georgie, "than all three of you put together. I could do it with my left hand!"

The three laughed bitingly in chorus. They jeered, derided, scoffed, and raised an uproar which would have had its effect upon much stronger nerves than Georgie's. For a time he contained his rising choler and chanted monotonously, over and over: "I COULD! I COULD, TOO! I COULD! I COULD, TOO!" But their tumult wore upon him, and he decided to avail himself of the recent decision whereby a big H was rendered innocuous and unprofane. Having used the expression once, he found it comforting, and substituted it for: "I could! I could, too!"

But it relieved him only temporarily. His tormentors were unaffected by it and increased their howlings, until at last Georgie lost his head altogether. Badgered beyond bearing, his eyes shining with a wild light, he broke through the besieging trio, hurling little Maurice from his path with a frantic hand.

"I'll show you!" he cried, in this sudden frenzy. "You give me a chance, and I'll prove it right NOW!"

"That's talkin' business!" shouted Penrod. "Everybody keep still a minute. Everybody!"

He took command of the situation at once, displaying a fine capacity for organization and system. It needed only a few minutes to set order in the place of confusion and to determine, with the full concurrence of all parties, the conditions under which Georgie Bassett was to defend his claim by undergoing what may be perhaps intelligibly defined as the Herman test. Georgie declared he could do it easily. He was in a state of great excitement and in no condition to think calmly or, probably, he would not have made the attempt at all. Certainly he was overconfident.

CHAPTER XXVII
CONCLUSION OF THE QUIET AFTERNOON

IT WAS DURING THE DISCUSSION OF the details of this enterprise that Georgie's mother, a short distance down the street, received a few female callers, who came by appointment to drink a glass of iced tea with her, and to meet the Rev. Mr. Kinosling. Mr. Kinosling was proving almost formidably interesting to the women and girls of his own and other flocks. What favour of his fellow clergymen a slight precociousness of manner and pronunciation cost him was more than balanced by the visible ecstasies of ladies. They blossomed at his touch.

He had just entered Mrs. Bassett's front door, when the son of the house, followed by an intent and earnest company of four, opened the alley gate and came into the yard. The unconscious Mrs. Bassett was about to have her first experience of a fatal coincidence. It was her first, because she was the mother of a boy so well behaved that he had become a proverb of transcendency. Fatal coincidences were plentiful in the Schofield and Williams families, and would have been familiar to Mrs. Bassett had Georgie been permitted greater intimacy with Penrod and Sam.

Mr. Kinosling sipped his iced tea and looked about, him approvingly. Seven ladies leaned forward, for it was to be seen that he meant to speak.

"This cool room is a relief," he said, waving a graceful hand in a neatly limited gesture, which everybody's eyes followed, his own included. "It is a relief and a retreat. The windows open, the blinds closed—that is as it should be. It is a retreat, a fastness, a bastion against the heat's assault. For me, a quiet room—a quiet room and a book, a volume in the hand, held lightly between the fingers. A volume of poems, lines metrical and cadenced; something by a sound Victorian. We have no later poets."

"Swinburne?" suggested Miss Beam, an eager spinster. "Swinburne, Mr. Kinosling? Ah, SWINBURNE!"

"Not Swinburne," said Mr. Kinosling chastely. "No."

That concluded all the remarks about Swinburne.

Miss Beam retired in confusion behind another lady; and somehow there became diffused an impression that Miss Beam was erotic.

"I do not observe your manly little son," Mr. Kinosling addressed his hostess.

"He's out playing in the yard," Mrs. Bassett returned. "I heard his voice just now, I think."

"Everywhere I hear wonderful report of him," said Mr. Kinosling. "I may say that I understand boys, and I feel that he is a rare, a fine, a pure, a lofty spirit. I say spirit, for spirit is the word I hear spoken of him."

A chorus of enthusiastic approbation affirmed the accuracy of this proclamation, and Mrs. Bassett flushed with pleasure. Georgie's spiritual perfection was demonstrated by instances of it, related by the visitors; his piety was cited, and wonderful things he had said were quoted.

"Not all boys are pure, of fine spirit, of high mind," said Mr. Kinosling, and continued with true feeling: "You have a neighbour, dear Mrs. Bassett, whose household I indeed really feel it quite impossible to visit until such time when better, firmer, stronger handed, more determined discipline shall prevail. I find Mr. and Mrs. Schofield and their daughter charming—"

Three or four ladies said "Oh!" and spoke a name simultaneously. It was as if they had said, "Oh, the bubonic plague!"

"Oh! Penrod Schofield!"

"Georgie does not play with him," said Mrs. Bassett quickly—"that is, he avoids him as much as he can without hurting Penrod's feelings. Georgie is very sensitive to giving pain. I suppose a mother should not tell these things, and I know people who talk about their own children are dreadful bores, but it was only last Thursday night that Georgie looked up in my face so sweetly, after he had said his prayers and his little cheeks flushed, as he said: 'Mamma, I think it would be right for me to go more with Penrod. I think it would make him a better boy.'"

A sibilance went about the room. "Sweet! How sweet! The sweet little soul! Ah, SWEET!"

"And that very afternoon," continued Mrs. Bassett, "he had come home in a dreadful state. Penrod had thrown tar all over him."

"Your son has a forgiving spirit!" said Mr. Kinosling with vehemence. "A too forgiving spirit, perhaps." He set down his glass. "No more, I thank you. No more cake, I thank you. Was it not Cardinal Newman who said—"

He was interrupted by the sounds of an altercation just outside the closed blinds of the window nearest him.

"Let him pick his tree!" It was the voice of Samuel Williams. "Didn't we come over here to give him one of his own trees? Give him a fair show, can't you?"

"The little lads!" Mr. Kinosling smiled. "They have their games, their outdoor sports, their pastimes. The young muscles are toughening. The sun will not harm them. They grow; they expand; they learn. They learn fair play, honour, courtesy, from one another, as pebbles grow round in the brook. They learn more from themselves than from us. They take shape, form, outline. Let them."

"Mr. Kinosling!" Another spinster—undeterred by what had happened to Miss Beam—leaned fair forward, her face shining and ardent. "Mr. Kinosling, there's a question I DO wish to ask you."

"My dear Miss Cosslit," Mr. Kinosling responded, again waving his hand and watching it, "I am entirely at your disposal."

"WAS Joan of Arc," she asked fervently, "inspired by spirits?"

He smiled indulgently. "Yes—and no," he said. "One must give both answers. One must give the answer, yes; one must give the answer, no."

"Oh, THANK you!" said Miss Cosslit, blushing.

"She's one of my great enthusiasms, you know."

"And I have a question, too," urged Mrs. Lora Rewbush, after a moment's hasty concentration. "'I've never been able to settle it for myself, but NOW—"

"Yes?" said Mr. Kinosling encouragingly.

"Is—ah—is—oh, yes: Is Sanskrit a more difficult language than Spanish, Mr. Kinosling?"

"It depends upon the student," replied the oracle smiling. "One must not look for linguists everywhere. In my own especial case—if one may cite one's self as an example—I found no great, no insurmountable difficulty in mastering, in conquering either."

"And may *I* ask one?" ventured Mrs. Bassett. "Do you think it is right to wear egrets?"

"There are marks of quality, of caste, of social distinction," Mr. Kinosling began, "which must be permitted, allowed, though perhaps regulated. Social distinction, one observes, almost invariably implies spiritual distinction as well. Distinction of circumstances is accompanied by mental distinction. Distinction is hereditary; it descends from father to son, and if there is one thing more true than 'Like father, like son,' it is—" he bowed gallantly to Mrs. Bassett—"it is, 'Like mother, like son.' What these good ladies have said this afternoon of YOUR—"

This was the fatal instant. There smote upon all ears the voice of Georgie, painfully shrill and penetrating—fraught with protest and protracted, strain. His plain words consisted of the newly sanctioned and disinfected curse with a big H.

With an ejaculation of horror, Mrs. Bassett sprang to the window and threw open the blinds.

Georgie's back was disclosed to the view of the tea-party. He was endeavouring to ascend a maple tree about twelve feet from the window. Embracing the trunk with arms and legs, he had managed to squirm to a point above the heads of Penrod and Herman, who stood close by, watching him earnestly—Penrod being obviously in charge of the performance. Across the yard were Sam Williams and Maurice Levy, acting as a jury on the question of voice-power, and it was to a complaint of theirs that Georgie had just replied.

"That's right, Georgie," said Penrod encouragingly. "They can, too, hear you. Let her go!"

"Going to heaven!" shrieked Georgie, squirming up another inch. "Going to heaven, heaven, heaven!"

His mother's frenzied attempts to attract his attention failed utterly. Georgie was using the full power of his lungs, deafening his own ears to all other sounds. Mrs. Bassett called in vain; while the tea-party stood petrified in a cluster about the window.

"Going to heaven!" Georgie bellowed. "Going to heaven! Going to heaven, my Lord! Going to heaven, heaven, heaven!"

He tried to climb higher, but began to slip downward, his exertions causing damage to his apparel. A button flew into the air, and his knickerbockers and his waistband severed relations.

"Devil's got my coat-tails, sinners! Old devil's got my coat-tails!" he announced appropriately. Then he began to slide.

He relaxed his clasp of the tree and slid to the ground.

"Going to hell!" shrieked Georgie, reaching a high pitch of enthusiasm in this great climax. "Going to hell! Going to hell! I'm gone to hell, hell, hell!"

With a loud scream, Mrs. Bassett threw herself out of the window, alighting by some miracle upon her feet with ankles unsprained.

Mr. Kinosling, feeling that his presence as spiritual adviser was demanded in the yard, followed with greater dignity through the front door. At the corner of the house a small departing figure collided with him violently. It was Penrod, tactfully withdrawing from what promised to be a family scene of unusual painfulness.

Mr. Kinosling seized him by the shoulders and, giving way to emotion, shook him viciously.

"You horrible boy!" exclaimed Mr. Kinosling. "You ruffianly creature! Do you know what's going to happen to you when you grow up? Do you realize what you're going to BE!"

With flashing eyes, the indignant boy made know his unshaken purpose. He shouted the reply:

"A minister!"

TO BE CONTINUED IN LITERARY OUTLAW #9

LINDA TURNER, HOLLYWOOD STAR AND AMERICA'S SWEETHEART, BECOMES BORED WITH HER ULTRA-SOPHISTICATED LIFE OF MOVIE MAKE-BELIEVE AND TAKES TO CRIME-FIGHTING IN HER MOST DRAMATIC ROLE OF ALL AS THE----
BLACK CAT
HOLLYWOOD'S GLAMOROUS DETECTIVE STAR
AN INNOCENT GIFT IS A KEY TO A MYSTERY SO AMAZING AS TO PROVOKE LINDA TURNER, TO DOFF HER ROLE AS HOLLYWOOD'S MOST GLAMOROUS ACTRESS FOR HER SECRET DISGUISE AS THE BLACK CAT..... WITH RICK HORNE, MOVIETOWN'S ACE NEWSHAWK, BLACK CAT PLUNGES INTO A MAZE OF ORIENTAL CUNNING AND BRUTALITY IN HER SEARCH TO DISCOVER ...
"THE BUDDHA'S SECRET"
LEE ELIAS

AT CENTURY STUDIOS, LINDA TURNER, GLAMOROUS HOLLYWOOD STAR, IS COMPLETING WORK ON HER LATEST PICTURE, "BLOOD ON THE IDOL"..
SPARE THE HOUSE OF LOO, O HOLY ONE! THEY HAVE PAID FOR THEIR SINS!

THE WRONG WAS GREAT BUT THE REPENTANCE GREATER ... A FULL LIFE SHALL BE THEIRS!
OUR DEEPEST GRATITUDE, O MIGHTY LORD!
CUT!

YOUR PORTRAYAL, MISS TURNER ... IT WAS PERFECT ... AS THOUGH YOU WERE A NATIVE CHINESE!
THANK YOU, FU CHU! IT WAS EASY WITH YOU TO GUIDE ME!

THIS IS A LOVELY PIECE, FU CHU! YOU MUST SELL IT TO ME!
IT SHALL BE YOURS, MY DEAR ... A GIFT FROM THE CHU IMPORTING HOUSE!
NOT THAT ONE, FATHER! IT IS SOLD! I BOUGHT IT IN CHINA FOR AN OLD CUSTOMER!

I HAVE SPOKEN, MY SON! YOUR PATRON SHALL HAVE ANOTHER BUDDHA FROM OUR SHOP! NOW GATHER OUR PROPS WE'VE LOANED THE STUDIO!
AS YOU SAY, MY FATHER!

THAT EVENING, LINDA RETURNS HOME FROM THE STUDIO ...
FU IS A GRAND MAN ... TAKES TIME FROM HIS IMPORTANT BUSINESS TO SERVE AS AN ADVISER TO THE STUDIO ... FURNISHES PROPS, EVEN ALLOWS HIS SON TO PLAY AN OCCASIONAL ROLE ....

TOBY, WHAT IS IT? SOMETHING IN THE NEXT ROOM?
HISSS!

THE BUDDHA! BUT WHY?

IT'S TIME BLACK CAT SWINGS INTO ACTION!

MINUTES LATER····
CHANG CHU'S MY FIRST CUSTOMER···HE ACTED MIGHTY STRANGE WHEN HIS FATHER GAVE ME THE BUDDHA TODAY!

AS NIGHT FALLS ON LOS ANGELES' CHINATOWN····
CHINA SH
CHOP SH

TO A DESERTED, EERIE SECTION
NOW TO SEE WHAT'S WHAT!
FU CHU CO IMPORTERS
CU ANTIQUES
FU CHU CO. IMPORTERS

BETTER GO IN THIS WAY!
FU CHU C
IMPORTER

MADE IT WITHOUT... OH... THOSE EYES... SOMEONE ELSE IN HERE... BETTER MOVE FAST!

SNEAKING QUIETLY BEHIND HER UNKNOWN FOE, BLACK CAT LUNGES AND GRASPS...
A BRONZE OWL! WELL, OF ALL THINGS!

GOING BELOW...
THIS PLACE WOULD GIVE A REAL CAT THE CREEPS!

OOOHH...
HA-HA-HO-HO-HO...

HA·HA·HA! THAT WAS WORTH A MONTH'S PAY! YOU WEREN'T SCARED FOR A MOMENT, WERE YOU?
RICK HORNE! AND WHAT IS HOLLYWOOD'S ACE REPORTER DOING HERE?

JUST CHECKING A TIP ON A SMUGGLING RACKET... AND YOU BEAUTEOUS BLACK CAT?
LISTEN! SCREAMS! SOMEONE'S IN TROUBLE... LET'S GO, RICK!

DASHING FROM THE CURIO SHOP, RICK AND BLACK CAT FIND THEMSELVES IN FU CHU'S GARDEN MUSEUM....
HEY, WAIT FOR ME!
HURRY, RICK! TO THE TEMPLE!
OOOW! HELP! MURDER!!

RUSHING ACROSS THE GARDEN THEY BREAK INTO THE TEMPLE....
YEEOW HELP! LET ME GO!
CHANG CHU, IF YOU WISH TO LIVE TELL ME WHERE THEY ARE HIDDEN!
I KNOW NOTHING! PLEASE.. MAKE HIM STOP! HE'S KILLING ME!

I'D BETTER GET TO THE BOTTOM OF THIS!
YEEO-OW! MERCY... I'M INNOCENT!

THIS GUY'S A ROCK OF GIBRALTER!
CONFEDER- ATES! LING, COME QUICKLY!

GIVE ME THE BRUSH-OFF, EH? WELL, WE SHALL SEE....
BLACK CAT... SAVE ME... IT'S MURDER!

MAYBE THIS WILL SIMMER YOU DOWN TO SIZE!

桌少!
THE BIGGER THEY COME...

THE HARDER THEY FALL! NOW TO UNTIE CHANG!
?

BO-O-Y-N-NG!

芳虫石裏!

中岛!
WOW! I CAN'T DENT THIS GUY!

UUGGHHH...
SHADES OF MY OLD LASSOING DAYS!

YOWEE! BULL'S EYE!
柔暴！
WHEW... THAT WAS CLOSE!

QUICK TO CAPITALIZE ON THE TONG'S SURPRISE, RICK PICKS UP THE GONG MALLET...

WOOFF!

THAT SHOULD RATE A GOOD CIGAR!
RICK...GET CHANG AND FOLLOW ME! THE OLD MAN'S SNEAKING OUT OF THE TEMPLE!

SWIFTFOOTED, STEALTHILY, LIKE HER NAMESAKE, BLACK CAT POUNCES!
HOLD ON, OLD TIMER! I WANT WORDS WITH YOU! WHAT'S YOUR RACKET?
RACKET? YOUR SPEECH IS STRANGE, O MASKED ONE! I, TENSIN, HIGH PRIEST OF TEN SIE, SEEK ONLY WHAT BELONGS TO MY GOD!

THIS MAN, CHANG CHU, SINNED GREATLY! HE STOLE THE RUBY EYES FROM THE IMAGE OF MY GOD! I FOLLOWED HIM FROM GREAT CHINA TO RECOVER THEM.... I HAVE FAILED! ONLY DISGRACE IS LEFT!

IS THIS TRUE, CHANG?
SURE ... I STOLE THEM AND HID THEM IN THIS BUDDHA-- EVERY TIME I WENT TO CHINA TO BUY CURIOS FOR MY FATHER I SMUGGLED JEWELS BACK IN THE MERCHANDISE!

I'M LEAVING NOW! I'LL SHOOT THE FIRST ONE WHO TRIES TO STOP ME!
PUT THE FIRE-STICK AWAY, MY SON! WE MUST RE-DEEM THE GOOD NAME OF CHU!
IT'S FU CHU! THE NOISE MUST HAVE AWAKENED HIM!

MY SON, MY SON! WHAT DEVIL POSSESSED YOU TO DO THESE GREAT WRONGS?
I GAMBLED...LOST HEAVILY--FEARED YOUR WRATH IF YOU LEARNED THE TRUTH.... TURNED TO SMUGGLING TO PAY OFF ROCKY SLADE ...

O, MIGHTY PROPHET, ACCEPT YOUR LOSS AND FORGIVE THE HOUSE OF CHU ITS SINS!
AWRIGHT, KNOCK OFF THE HEARTS AND FLOWERS OUT THERE!

ROCKY SLADE!
YEAH, KID! I GOT TIRED WAITIN' AN' I FIGURED YOU MIGHT TRY AN OLD DOUBLE-CROSS ON ROCKY! NOW I'LL TAKE THE ICE!
'DON'T NONE OF YOUSE TRY NUTTIN', SEE?

YOU SHALL NOT HAVE THIS... AAAGHH...
PUT THE OLD GOAT OUT OF THE WAY, SLUG!

CHECK ROCKY!
SPARE MY FATHER! HE'S A GOOD MAN! IT WAS I... AIGHAA...

BLACK CAT, QUICK TO TAKE ADVANTAGE OF THE DISTRACTION CAUSED BY CHANG, SWINGS INTO ACTION·····
I GOT THE STUFF, BOYS! LET'S BLOW!
NOT SO FAST, 'CAUSE...

...I'M FASTER!
HEY! WOT DA...

UUGGH!
YEOWEE!
THANKS FOR SETTING 'EM UP, BLACK CAT!

DIS'LL STOP YA!
SUCH MANNERS!

NEVER TRY TO HIT A LADY FROM BEHIND!
YIPE!
STAY DOWN, BABY! LEAD'S ABOUT TO FLY!

WOW! THAT WAS CLOSE!
BUT NOT CLOSE ENOUGH!

THAT'S THE LAST ONE! BETTER SEE IF I CAN HELP CHANG!

ALL IS FORGIVEN, MY SON... YOU HAVE WASHED THE STAINS FROM THE HOUSE OF CHU!
THANK YOU... FATHER-- I DIE-- HAPPY...
THE EYES... THEY ARE NOT HERE!

THE NEXT DAY, AT THE TURNER HOME, RICK HORNE DESCRIBES HIS LATEST ADVENTURES WITH BLACK CAT TO LINDA AND TIM TURNER ....
...AND THEY NEVER DID FIND THE JEWELS! BUT THE BLACK CAT WAS TERRIFIC! SHE'S THE KIND OF GIRL I'D LIKE TO KNOW BETTER!
GOSH! BLACK CAT LEADS AN EXCITING LIFE! I WISH I HAD THE COURAGE TO DO SOME OF THOSE THINGS!
IS THAT SO, DAUGHTER?

MEOWRR!
BUT THAT'S NOT FOR YOU! YOU'RE NOT THE TYPE!
TOBY! BE CAREFUL! MY BUDDHA-- OOOH!

LINDA! LOOK! THE EYES OF TENSIE!
WHY... WHY CHANG MUST HAVE BROUGHT THEM HERE BY MISTAKE WHEN HE TOOK MY OTHER BUDDHA AND REPLACED IT WITH THIS ONE!

WOW! THERE'S A TWIST TO MY STORY'S ENDING! BYE, NOW!-- GOTTA GO POUND THE TYPEWRITER!
BYE, RICKY, DEAR!
SO LONG, RICK..

THAT WAS NICE GOING, BLACK CAT -- ER, LINDA!
GLAD YOU APPROVE, POPS! THAT RICK HORNE'S SURE CUTE! BUT OF COURSE --

YOU'RE THE ONLY ONE THAT KNOWS WHAT'S BENEATH LINDA TURNER'S GLAMOROUS GET-UPS!
YOUR SECRET'S SAFE WITH YOUR DAD, LINDA! YOU'VE PICKED THIS BLACK CAT JOB FOR YOURSELF AND I'M PROUD OF YOU!

AS LONG AS THERE'S TROUBLE IN HOLLYWOOD-- BLACK CAT WILL BE AROUND FOR ACTION!

DON'T MISS the BIG 4th ISSUE

CAN THE BLACK CAT SOLVE THE MYSTERY OF THE "GHOST OF BLASCO"? A RIP-ROARING SUSPENSE- FILLED YARN WITH ALL THE GLAMOUR OF THE HOLLYWOOD STAGE FOR BACKGROUND...

HOLLYWOOD'S GLAMOROUS DETECTIVE STAR
BLACK CAT NO. 4
BLACK CAT COMICS 10¢

ON SALE XMAS A BIG 10¢ WORTH!

BEREFT

Where had I heard this wind before
Change like this to a deeper roar?
What would it take my standing there for,
Holding open a restive door,
Looking down hill to a frothy shore?
Summer was past and the day was past.
Sombre clouds in the west were massed.
Out on the porch's sagging floor,
Leaves got up in a coil and hissed,
Blindly struck at my knee and missed.
Something sinister in the tone
Told me my secret must be known:
Word I was in the house alone
Somehow must have gotten abroad,
Word I was in my life alone,
Word I had no one left but God.

— Robert Frost, 1928

THE WIVES OF THE DEAD

BY NATHANIEL HAWTHORNE

THE FOLLOWING STORY, THE SIMPLE and domestic incidents of which may be deemed scarcely worth relating, after such a lapse of time, awakened some degree of interest, a hundred years ago, in a principal seaport of the Bay Province. The rainy twilight of an autumn day,—a parlor on the second floor of a small house, plainly furnished, as beseemed the middling circumstances of its inhabitants, yet decorated with little curiosities from beyond the sea, and a few delicate specimens of Indian manufacture,— these are the only particulars to be premised in regard to scene and season. Two young and comely women sat together by the fireside, nursing their mutual and peculiar sorrows. They were the recent brides of two brothers, a sailor and a landsman, and two successive days had brought tidings of the death of each, by the chances of Canadian warfare and the tempestuous Atlantic. The universal sympathy excited by this bereavement drew numerous condoling guests to the habitation of the widowed sisters. Several, among whom was the minister, had remained till the verge of evening; when, one by one, whispering many comfortable passages of Scripture, that were answered by more abundant tears, they took their leave, and departed to their own happier homes. The mourners, though not insensible to the kindness of their friends, had yearned to be left alone. United, as they had been, by the relationship of the living, and now more closely so by that of the dead, each felt as if whatever consolation her grief admitted were to be found in the bosom of the other. They joined their hearts, and wept together silently. But after an hour of such indulgence, one of the sisters, all of whose emotions were influenced by her mild, quiet, yet not feeble character, began to recollect the precepts of resignation and endurance which piety had taught her, when she did not think to need them. Her misfortune, besides, as earliest known, should earliest cease to interfere with her regular course of duties; accordingly, having placed the table before the fire, and arranged a frugal meal, she took the hand of her companion.

"Come, dearest sister; you have eaten not a morsel to-day," she said. "Arise, I pray you, and let us ask a blessing on that which is provided for us."

Her sister-in-law was of a lively and irritable temperament, and the first pangs of her sorrow had been expressed by shrieks and passionate lamentation. She now shrunk from Mary's words, like a wounded sufferer from a hand that revives the throb.

"There is no blessing left for me, neither will I ask it!" cried Margaret, with a fresh burst of tears. "Would it were His will that I might never taste food more!"

Yet she trembled at these rebellious expressions, almost as soon as they were uttered, and, by degrees, Mary succeeded in bringing her sister's mind nearer to the situation of her own. Time went on, and their usual hour of repose arrived. The brothers and their brides, entering the married state with no more than the slender means which then sanctioned such a step, had confederated themselves in one household, with equal rights to the parlor, and claiming exclusive privileges in two sleeping-rooms contiguous to it. Thither the widowed ones retired, after heaping ashes upon the dying embers of their fire, and placing a lighted lamp upon the hearth. The doors of both chambers were left open, so that a part of the interior of each, and the beds with their unclosed curtains, were reciprocally visible. Sleep did not steal upon the sisters at one and the same time. Mary experienced the effect often consequent upon grief quietly borne, and soon sunk into temporary forgetfulness, while Margaret became more disturbed and feverish, in proportion as the night advanced with its deepest and stillest hours. She lay listening to the drops of rain, that came down in monotonous succession, unswayed by a breath of wind; and a nervous impulse continually caused her to lift her head from the pillow, and gaze into Mary's chamber and the intermediate apartment. The cold light of the lamp threw the shadows of the furniture up against the wall, stamping them immovably there, except when they were shaken by a sudden flicker of the flame. Two vacant arm-chairs were in their old positions on opposite sides of the hearth, where the brothers had been wont to sit in young and laughing dignity, as heads of families; two humbler seats were near them, the true thrones of that little empire, where Mary and herself had exercised in love a power that love had won. The cheerful radiance of the fire had shone upon the happy circle, and the dead glimmer of the lamp might have befitted their reunion now. While Margaret groaned in bitterness, she heard a knock at the street door.

"How would my heart have leapt at that sound but yesterday!" thought she, remembering the anxiety with which she had long awaited tidings from her husband.

"I care not for it now; let them begone, for I will not arise."

But even while a sort of childish fretfulness made her thus resolve, she was breathing hurriedly, and straining her ears to catch a repetition of the summons. It is difficult to be convinced of the death of one whom we have deemed another self. The knocking was now renewed in slow and regular strokes, apparently given with the soft end of a doubled fist, and was accompanied by words, faintly heard through several thicknesses of wall. Margaret looked to her sister's chamber, and beheld her still lying in the depths of sleep. She arose, placed her foot upon the floor, and slightly arrayed herself, trembling between fear and eagerness as she did so.

"Heaven help me!" sighed she. "I have nothing left to fear, and methinks I am ten times more a coward than ever."

Seizing the lamp from the hearth, she hastened to the window that overlooked the street-door. It was a lattice, turning upon hinges; and having thrown it back, she stretched her head a little way into the moist atmosphere. A lantern was reddening the front of the house, and melting its light in the neighboring puddles, while a deluge of darkness overwhelmed every other object. As the window grated on its hinges, a man in a broad-brimmed hat and blanket-coat stepped from under the shelter of the projecting story, and looked upward to discover whom his application had aroused. Margaret knew him as a friendly innkeeper of the town.

"What would you have, Goodman Parker?" cried the widow.

"Lackaday, is it you, Mistress Margaret?" replied the innkeeper. "I was afraid it might be your sister Mary; for I hate to see a young woman in trouble, when I have n't a word of comfort to whisper her."

"For Heaven's sake, what news do you bring?" screamed Margaret.

"Why, there has been an express through the town within this half-hour," said Goodman Parker, "travelling from the eastern jurisdiction with letters from the governor and council. He tarried at my house to refresh himself with a drop and a morsel, and I asked him what tidings on the frontiers. He tells me we had the better in the skirmish you wot of, and that thirteen men reported slain are well and sound, and your husband among them. Besides, he is appointed of the escort to bring the captivated Frenchers and Indians home to the province jail. I judged you would n't mind being broke of your rest, and so I stepped over to tell you. Good night."

So saying, the honest man departed; and his lantern gleamed along the street, bringing to view indistinct shapes of things, and the fragments of a world, like order glimmering through chaos, or memory roaming over the past. But Margaret stayed not to watch these picturesque effects. Joy flashed into her heart, and lighted it up at once; and breathless, and with winged steps, she flew to the bedside of her sister. She paused, however, at the door of the chamber, while a thought of pain broke in upon her.

"Poor Mary!" said she to herself. "Shall I waken her, to feel her sorrow sharpened by my happiness? No; I will keep it within my own bosom till the morrow."

She approached the bed, to discover if Mary's sleep were peaceful. Her face was turned partly inward to the pillow, and had been hidden there to weep; but a look of motionless contentment was now visible upon it, as if her heart, like a deep lake, had grown calm because its dead had sunk down so far within. Happy is it, and strange, that the lighter sorrows are those from which dreams are chiefly fabricated. Margaret shrunk from disturbing her sister-in-law, and felt as if her own better fortune had rendered her involuntarily unfaithful, and as if altered and diminished affection must be the consequence of the disclosure she had to make. With a sudden step she turned away. But joy could not long be repressed, even by circumstances that would have excited heavy grief at another moment. Her mind was thronged with delightful thoughts, till sleep stole on, and transformed them to visions, more delightful and more wild, like the breath of winter (but what a cold comparison!) working fantastic tracery upon a window.

When the night was far advanced, Mary awoke with a sudden start. A vivid dream had latterly involved her in its unreal life, of which, however, she could only remember that it had been broken in upon at the most interesting point. For a little time, slumber hung about her like a morning mist, hindering her from perceiving the distinct outline of her situation. She listened with imperfect consciousness to two or three volleys of a rapid and eager knocking; and first she deemed the noise a matter of course, like the breath she drew; next, it appeared a thing in which she had no concern; and lastly, she became aware that it was a summons necessary to be obeyed. At the same moment, the pang of recollection darted into her mind; the pall of sleep was thrown back from the face of grief; the dim light of the chamber, and the objects therein revealed, had retained all her suspended ideas, and restored them as soon as she unclosed her eyes. Again there was a quick peal upon the street-door. Fearing that her sister would also be disturbed, Mary wrapped herself in a cloak and hood, took the lamp from the hearth, and hastened to the window. By some accident, it had been left unhasped, and yielded easily to her hand.

"Who's there?" asked Mary, trembling as she looked forth.

The storm was over, and the moon was up; it shone upon broken clouds above, and below upon houses black with moisture, and upon little lakes of the fallen rain, curling into silver beneath the quick enchantment of a breeze. A young man in a sailor's dress, wet as if he had come out of the depths of the sea, stood alone under the window. Mary recognized him as one whose livelihood was gained by short voyages along the coast; nor did she forget that, previous to her marriage, he had been an unsuccessful wooer of her own.

"What do you seek here, Stephen?" said she.

"Cheer up, Mary, for I seek to comfort you," answered the rejected lover. "You must know I got home not ten minutes ago, and the first thing my good mother told me was the news about your husband. So, without saying a word to the old woman, I clapped on my hat, and ran out of the house. I could n't have slept a wink before speaking to you, Mary, for the sake of old times."

"Stephen, I thought better of you!" exclaimed the widow, with gushing tears and preparing to close the lattice; for she was no whit inclined to imitate the first wife of Zadig.

"But stop, and hear my story out," cried the young sailor. "I tell you we spoke a brig yesterday afternoon, bound in from Old England. And who do you think I saw standing on deck, well and hearty, only a bit thinner than he was five months ago?"

Mary leaned from the window, but could not speak. "Why, it was your husband himself," continued the generous seaman. "He and three others saved themselves on a spar, when the Blessing turned bottom upwards. The brig will beat into the bay by daylight, with this wind, and you'll see him here to-morrow. There's the comfort I bring you, Mary, and so good night."

He hurried away, while Mary watched him with a doubt of waking reality, that seemed stronger or weaker as he alternately entered the shade of the houses, or emerged into the broad streaks of moonlight. Gradually, however, a blessed flood of conviction swelled into her heart, in strength enough to overwhelm her, had its increase been more abrupt. Her first impulse was to rouse her sister-in-law, and communicate the new-born gladness. She opened the chamber-door, which had been closed in the course of the night, though not latched, advanced to the bedside, and was about to lay her hand upon the slumberer's shoulder. But then she remembered that Margaret would awake to thoughts of death and woe, rendered not the less bitter by their contrast with her own felicity. She suffered the rays of the lamp to fall upon the unconscious form of the bereaved one. Margaret lay in unquiet sleep, and the drapery was displaced around her; her young cheek was rosy-tinted, and her lips half opened in a vivid smile; an expression of joy, debarred its passage by her sealed eyelids, struggled forth like incense from the whole countenance.

"My poor sister! you will waken too soon from that happy dream," thought Mary.

Before retiring, she set down the lamp, and endeavored to arrange the bedclothes so that the chill air might not do harm to the feverish slumberer. But her hand trembled against Margaret's neck, a tear also fell upon her cheek, and she suddenly awoke.

THE END

"MOONLIGHT IS SCULPTURE; SUNLIGHT IS PAINTING."

"EVERY INDIVIDUAL HAS A PLACE TO FILL IN THE WORLD AND IS IMPORTANT IN SOME RESPECT, WHETHER HE CHOOSES TO BE SO OR NOT."

— NATHANIEL HAWTHORNE

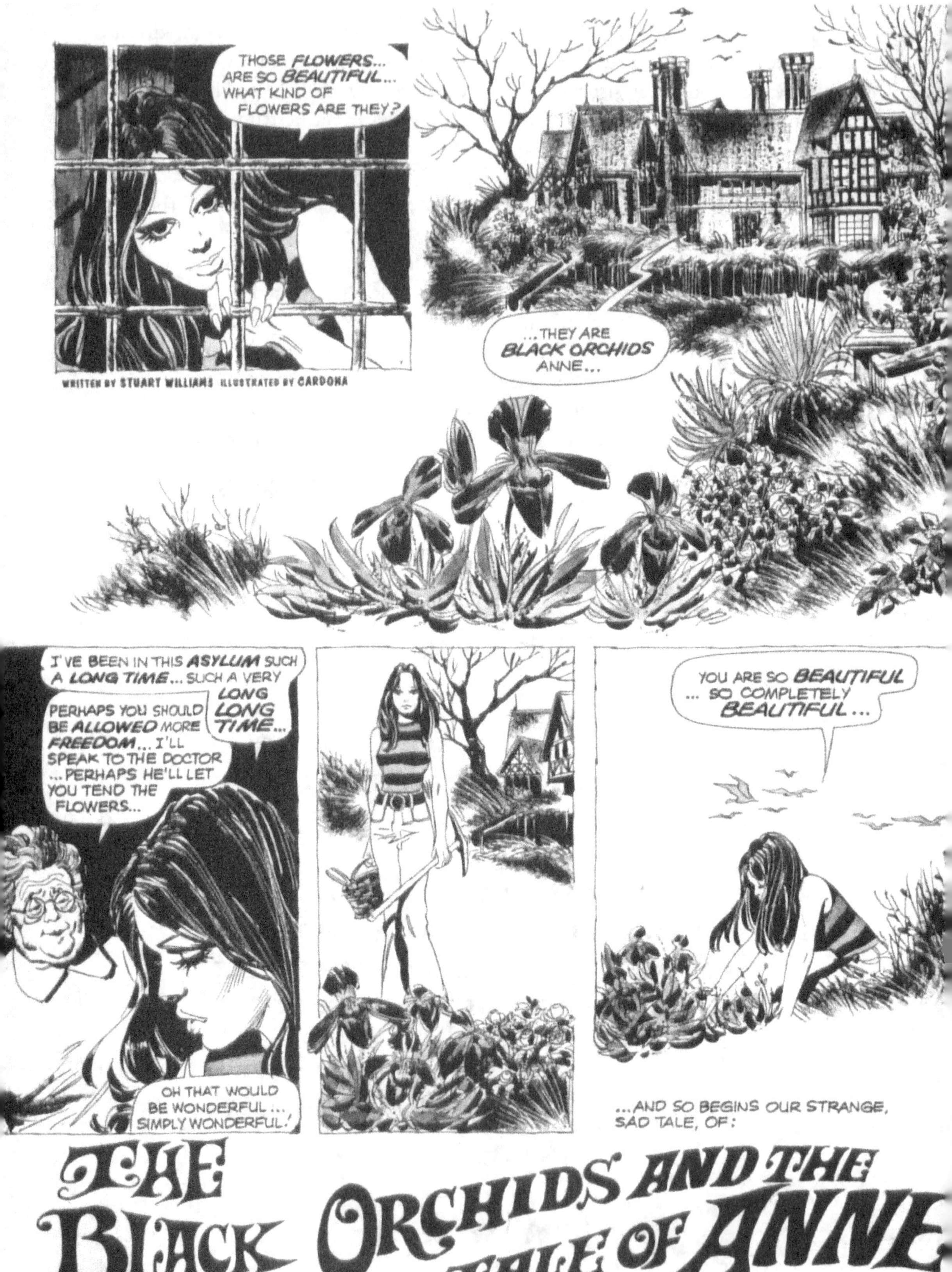

THE BLACK ORCHIDS AND THE TALE OF ANNE

YOU ARE SO... BEAUTIFUL!
SO BEAUTIFUL... SO DAMN BLOODY BEAUTIFUL!
SO DAMN BEAUTIFUL... SO DAMN DAMN BEAUTIFUL!
SO DAMN BEAUTIFUL!
I THOUGHT... SHE WAS GETTING WELL... I THOUGHT SHE WAS OVER IT...
I THOUGHT SO TOO MATRON... BUT APPARENTLY NOT! SHE IS VERY DISTURBED... THAT GIRL... VERY DISTURBED... I DON'T KNOW IF SHE'LL EVER GET OVER IT...

HER CASE IS VERY SAD... DO YOU KNOW HER HISTORY?
I KNOW A LITTLE ABOUT IT...
...IT'S PRETTY HIDEOUS...
SHE FOUND HER HUSBAND WITH A WOMAN...

...AND... SHE TOOK AN AXE, FIRST TO HER...
...THEN TO HIM...

"...WHEN THE POLICE CAME... SHE WAS WHISPERING BESIDE A TREE... THE AXE ON THE GROUND BESIDE HER ...AND NEARBY THE MUTILATED BODIES OF THE HUSBAND AND THE 'OTHER' WOMAN..."
OF COURSE, THE COURTS FOUND HER INSANE, VERY... 'DISTURBED', AND COMMITTED HER TO THIS ASYLUM FOR THE CRIMINALLY INSANE...
...IT... WAS A BIT OF AN OVER-REACTION, WASN'T IT?... I MEAN, TO FIND HER HUSBAND AND THE OTHER WOMAN SHOULDN'T NORMALLY BE ENOUGH TO PROVOKE A MURDER... SHE MUST'VE BEEN DEEPLY DISTURBED BEFORE THEN...
YES...WELL I ASSUME SHE WAS! UNDER CLINICAL HYPNOSIS, WE DISCOVERED THE WHOLE STORY...
...APPARENTLY THE 'OTHER' WOMAN WAS HER SISTER...
"...AND APPARENTLY, SHE WAS NOT A BEAUTIFUL GIRL, LIKE ANNE..."
"...ANNE WAS ALWAYS THE GIRL WITH BOY FRIENDS AND MANY DATES... WHILE HER SISTER MARY WAS ALONE AND WITHOUT MALE ADMIRERS..."

"...ANNE...DIDN'T THINK TOO MUCH ABOUT HER SISTER, AND CERTAINLY DIDN'T EVER SHOW THAT SHE CARED... SHE WAS NOT CRUEL, BUT SHE WAS CERTAINLY NOT 'NICE'... AND SO MARY CAME TO RESENT HER ATTRACTIVE SISTER, AND CAME TO FEEL VERY INSECURE..."

"...WELL, IN DUE COURSE, ANNE MARRIED...THE GUY SHE MARRIED WAS VERY MUCH IN LOVE WITH ANNE, AND WHAT YOU'D CALL A 'NICE GUY'!... SO WHEN MARY CAME TO THE HOUSE HE WAS 'FRIENDLY' WITH HER... AND HE BEING THE FIRST MAN MARY HAD ANY CONTACT WITH, SHE FELL IN LOVE WITH HIM..."

"...SHE POURED OUT HER HEART TO HIM, NOT BY WORDS, BUT BY ACTIONS, AND HE CAME TO REALIZE THAT SHE WAS A BEAUTIFUL GIRL INSIDE, WHILE HIS WIFE ANNE WAS BEAUTIFUL OUTSIDE..."

"...WELL, THE LONG OF SHORT OF IT IS, THAT THERE GREW BETWEEN JOHN MARSTON AND MARY AN EMOTIONAL LOVE, AND BETWEEN JOHN MARTSON AND HIS WIFE ANNE A PURELY PHYSICAL LOVE..."

"...AND THEN...ONE DAY..."
...MARY... I LOVE YOU... OH GOD I LOVE YOU...
...AND I LOVE YOU JOHN...BUT... BUT WHAT ABOUT ANNE?
YOU... DON'T UNDERSTAND MARY... I LOVE ANNE TOO... BUT IN A DIFFERENT WAY...

...IN A DIFFERENT WAY... I KNOW WHAT WAY... SHE IS BEAUTIFUL AND I...
...I AM NOT!!

OH BUT YOU ARE BEAUTIFUL MARY... INSIDE... ANNE IS BEAUTIFUL ONLY ON THE OUTSIDE—A SURFACE BEAUTY...
...BUT YOU I LOVE BECAUSE OF YOUR INNER BEAUTY...
OH LORD...
...THEY TALK OF ME AS IF I WERE... SO UGLY INSIDE... BUT I'M NOT... I'M NOT...

'...SO ANNE, WHOSE INSECURITIES AND CONFLICT WITH HER SISTER HAD, IN THE YEARS OF THEIR ADOLESCENCE, BEEN UNCONSCIOUS AND VERY SUBLIMINAL, NOW BECAME DRAMATIZED BY THE CONVERSATION SHE OVERHEAD AND...

--AND SHE JUST WENT BERSERK!!...."

...THAT'S IT... THAT'S ALL??
YES...THAT'S ALL... YOU SEE... FOR YEARS AND YEARS ANNE INDEED HAD ENVIED HER SISTER, AND DESPISED HER OWN BEAUTY BECAUSE SHE DID FEEL SORRY FOR MARY--AND WISHED HER SISTER HAD PHYSICAL BEAUTY TOO...
...BUT SHE WOULDN'T OR COULDN'T ADMIT IT--SO HER FRUSTRATION VENTED ITSELF IN THEIR MURDER...
ANNE... HATES... BEAUTY...

THERE ARE NO MIRRORS ANYWHERE NEAR... IF SHE SAW HER REFLECTION IN A MIRROR IT WOULD HAVE AN AWFUL EFFECT... SHE WOULD SEE HERSELF AS BEAUTIFUL, AND SOMEHOW TRY TO DESTROY IT...
...AS SHE DESTROYED HER 'BEAUTIFUL' SISTER --AND THE 'BEAUTIFUL' BLACK ORCHIDS...
...SO... MATRON, LET US PRAY... THAT SHE NEVER SEES HER OWN BEAUTY WHILE SEE IS STILL SO... DISTURBED...

NOW... WAIT HERE A MOMENT... I'LL BE RIGHT BACK...
...WAIT HERE ...ALRIGHT?
YES... I'LL WAIT...

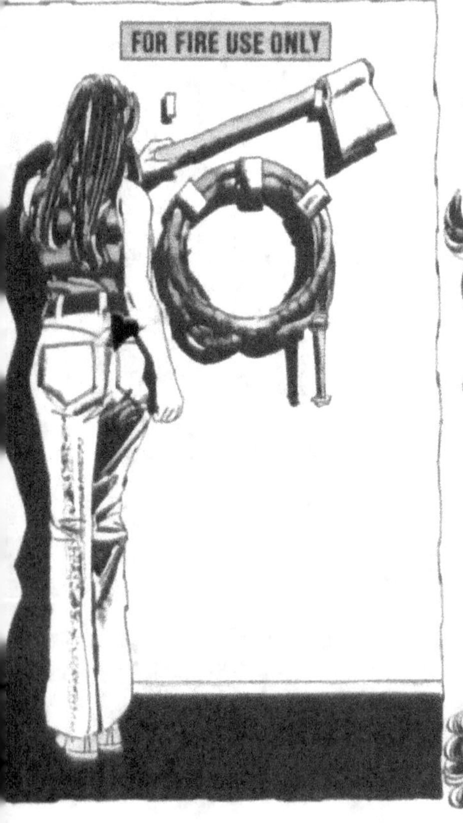
FOR FIRE USE ONLY

...THE BLACK ORCHIDS AND ANNE -- MAY THEY REST IN PEACE...

THE SKULL

BY PHILIP K. DICK

"What is this opportunity?" Conger asked. "Go on. I'm interested."

The room was silent; all faces were fixed on Conger—still in the drab prison uniform. The Speaker leaned forward slowly.

"Before you went to prison your trading business was paying well—all illegal—all very profitable. Now you have nothing, except the prospect of another six years in a cell."

Conger scowled.

"There is a certain situation, very important to this Council, that requires your peculiar abilities. Also, it is a situation you might find interesting. You were a hunter, were you not? You've done a great deal of trapping, hiding in the bushes, waiting at night for the game? I imagine hunting must be a source of satisfaction to you, the chase, the stalking—»

Conger sighed. His lips twisted. "All right," he said. "Leave that out. Get to the point. Who do you want me to kill?"

The Speaker smiled. "All in proper sequence," he said softly.

★ ★ ★

The car slid to a stop. It was night; there was no light anywhere along the street. Conger looked out. "Where are we? What is this place?"

The hand of the guard pressed into his arm. "Come. Through that door."

Conger stepped down, onto the damp sidewalk. The guard came swiftly after him, and then the Speaker. Conger took a deep breath of the cold air. He studied the dim outline of the building rising up before them.

"I know this place. I've seen it before." He squinted, his eyes growing accustomed to the dark. Suddenly he became alert. "This is—»

"Yes. The First Church." The Speaker walked toward the steps. "We're expected."

"Expected? *Here?*»

"Yes." The Speaker mounted the stairs. "You know we're not allowed in their Churches, especially with guns!" He stopped. Two armed soldiers loomed up ahead, one on each side.

"All right?" The Speaker looked up at them. They nodded. The door of the Church was open. Conger could see other soldiers inside, standing about, young soldiers with large eyes, gazing at the ikons and holy images.

"I see," he said.

"It was necessary," the Speaker said. "As you know, we have been singularly unfortunate in the past in our relations with the First Church."

"This won't help."

"But it's worth it. You will see."

★ ★ ★

THEY PASSED THROUGH THE HALL and into the main chamber where the altar piece was, and the kneeling places. The Speaker scarcely glanced at the altar as they passed by. He pushed open a small side door and beckoned Conger through.

"In here. We have to hurry. The faithful will be flocking in soon."

Conger entered, blinking. They were in a small chamber, low-ceilinged, with dark panels of old wood. There was a smell of ashes and smoldering spices in the room. He sniffed. "What's that? The smell."

"Cups on the wall. I don't know." The Speaker crossed impatiently to the far side. "According to our information, it is hidden here by this—»

Conger looked around the room. He saw books and papers, holy signs and images. A strange low shiver went through him.

"Does my job involve anyone of the Church? If it does—»

The Speaker turned, astonished. "Can it be that you believe in the Founder? Is it possible, a hunter, a killer—»

"No. Of course not. All their business about resignation to death, non-violence—»

"What is it, then?"

Conger shrugged. "I've been taught not to mix with such as these. They have strange abilities. And you can't reason with them."

The Speaker studied Conger thoughtfully. "You have the wrong idea. It is no one here that we have in mind. We've found that killing them only tends to increase their numbers."

"Then why come here? Let's leave."

"No. We came for something important. Something you will need to identify your man. Without it you won't be able to find him." A trace of a smile crossed the Speaker's face. "We don't want you to kill the wrong person. It's too important."

"I don't make mistakes." Conger's chest rose. "Listen, Speaker—»

"This is an unusual situation," the Speaker said. "You see, the person you are after—the person that we are sending you to find—is known only by certain objects here. They are the only traces, the only means of identification. Without them—»

"What are they?"

He came toward the Speaker. The Speaker moved to one side. "Look," he said. He drew a sliding wall away, showing a dark square hole. "In there."

Conger squatted down, staring in. He frowned. "A skull! A skeleton!"

"The man you are after has been dead for two centuries," the Speaker said. "This is all that remains of him. And this is all you have with which to find him."

For a long time Conger said nothing. He stared down at the bones, dimly visible in the recess of the wall. How could a man dead centuries be killed? How could he be stalked, brought down?

Conger was a hunter, a man who had lived as he pleased, where he pleased. He had kept himself alive by trading, bringing furs and pelts in from the Provinces on his own ship, riding at high speed, slipping through the customs line around Earth.

He had hunted in the great mountains of the moon. He had stalked through empty Martian cities. He had explored—

The Speaker said, "Soldier, take these objects and have them carried to the car. Don't lose any part of them."

The soldier went into the cupboard, reaching gingerly, squatting on his heels.

"It is my hope," the Speaker continued softly, to Conger, "that you will demonstrate your loyalty to us, now. There are always ways for citizens to restore themselves, to show their devotion to their society. For you I think this would be a very good chance. I seriously doubt that a better one will come. And for your efforts there will be quite a restitution, of course."

The two men looked at each other; Conger, thin, unkempt, the Speaker immaculate in his uniform.

"I understand you," Conger said. "I mean, I understand this part, about the chance. But how can a man who has been dead two centuries be—»

"I'll explain later," the Speaker said. "Right now we have to hurry!" The soldier had gone out with the bones, wrapped in a blanket held carefully in his arms. The Speaker walked to the door. "Come. They've already discovered that we've broken in here, and they'll be coming at any moment."

They hurried down the damp steps to the waiting car. A second later the driver lifted the car up into the air, above the house-tops.

The Speaker settled back in the seat.

"The First Church has an interesting past," he said. "I suppose you are familiar with it, but I'd like to speak of a few points that are of relevancy to us.

"It was in the twentieth century that the Movement began—during one of the periodic wars. The Movement developed rapidly, feeding on the general sense of futility, the realization that each war was breeding greater war, with no end in sight. The Movement posed a simple answer to the problem: Without military preparations—weapons—there could be no war. And without machinery and complex scientific technocracy there could be no weapons.

"The Movement preached that you couldn't stop war by planning for it. They preached that man was losing to his machinery and science, that it was getting away from him, pushing him into greater and greater wars. Down with society, they shouted. Down with factories and science! A few more wars and there wouldn't be much left of the world.

"The Founder was an obscure person from a small town in the American Middle West. We don't even know his name. All we know is that one day he appeared, preaching a doctrine of non-violence, non-resistance; no fighting, no paying taxes for guns, no research except for medicine. Live out your life quietly, tending your garden, staying out of public affairs; mind your own business. Be obscure, unknown, poor. Give away most of your possessions, leave the city. At least that was what developed from what he told the people."

The car dropped down and landed on a roof.

"The Founder preached this doctrine, or the germ of it; there's no telling how much the faithful have added themselves. The local authorities picked him up at once, of course. Apparently they were convinced that he meant it; he was never released. He was put to death, and his body buried secretly. It seemed that the cult was finished."

The Speaker smiled. "Unfortunately, some of his disciples reported seeing him after the date of his death. The rumor spread; he had conquered death, he was divine. It took hold, grew. And here we are today, with a First Church, obstructing all social progress, destroying society, sowing the seeds of anarchy—»

"But the wars," Conger said. "About them?"

"The wars? Well, there were no more wars. It must be acknowledged that the elimination of war was the direct result of non-violence practiced on a general scale. But we can take a more objective view of war today. What was so terrible about it? War had a profound selective value, perfectly in accord with the teachings of Darwin and Mendel and others. Without war the mass of useless, incompetent mankind, without training or intelligence, is permitted to grow and expand unchecked. War acted to reduce their numbers; like storms and earthquakes and droughts, it was nature's way of eliminating the unfit.

"Without war the lower elements of mankind have increased all out of proportion. They threaten the educated few, those with scientific knowledge and training, the ones equipped to direct society. They have no regard for science or a scientific society, based on reason. And this Movement seeks to aid and abet them. Only when scientists are in full control can the—»

★ ★ ★

HE LOOKED AT HIS WATCH AND THEN kicked the car door open. "I'll tell you the rest as we walk."

They crossed the dark roof. "Doubtless you now know whom those bones belonged to, who it is that we are after. He has been dead just two centuries, now, this ignorant man from the Middle West, this Founder. The tragedy is that the authorities of the time acted too slowly. They allowed him to speak, to get his message across. He was allowed to preach, to start his cult. And once such a thing is under way, there's no stopping it.

"But what if he had died before he preached? What if none of his doctrines had ever been spoken? It took only a moment for him to utter them, that we know. They say he spoke just once, just one time. *Then* the authorities came, taking him away. He offered no resistance; the incident was small."

The Speaker turned to Conger.

"Small, but we're reaping the consequences of it today."

They went inside the building. Inside, the soldiers had already laid out the skeleton on a table. The soldiers stood around it, their young faces intense.

Conger went over to the table, pushing past them. He bent down, staring at the bones. "So these are his remains," he murmured. "The Founder. The Church has hidden them for two centuries."

"Quite so," the Speaker said. "But now we have them. Come along down the hall."

They went across the room to a door. The Speaker pushed it open. Technicians looked up. Conger saw machinery, whirring and turning;

benches and retorts. In the center of the room was a gleaming crystal cage.

The Speaker handed a Slem-gun to Conger. "The important thing to remember is that the skull must be saved and brought back—for comparison and proof. Aim low—at the chest."

Conger weighed the gun in his hands. "It feels good," he said. "I know this gun—that is, I've seen them before, but I never used one."

The Speaker nodded. "You will be instructed on the use of the gun and the operation of the cage. You will be given all data we have on the time and location. The exact spot was a place called Hudson's field. About 1960 in a small community outside Denver, Colorado. And don't forget—the only means of identification you will have will be the skull. There are visible characteristics of the front teeth, especially the left incisor—»

Conger listened absently. He was watching two men in white carefully wrapping the skull in a plastic bag. They tied it and carried it into the crystal cage. "And if I should make a mistake?"

"Pick the wrong man? Then find the right one. Don't come back until you succeed in reaching this Founder. And you can't wait for him to start speaking; that's what we must avoid! You must act in advance. Take chances; shoot as soon as you think you've found him. He'll be someone unusual, probably a stranger in the area. Apparently he wasn't known."

Conger listened dimly.

"Do you think you have it all now?" the Speaker asked.

"Yes. I think so." Conger entered the crystal cage and sat down, placing his hands on the wheel.

"Good luck," the Speaker said. "We'll be awaiting the outcome. There's some philosophical doubt as to whether one can alter the past. This should answer the question once and for all."

Conger fingered the controls of the cage.

"By the way," the Speaker said. "Don't try to use this cage for purposes not anticipated in your job. We have a constant trace on it. If we want it back, we can get it back. Good luck."

Conger said nothing. The cage was sealed. He raised his finger and touched the wheel control. He turned the wheel carefully.

He was still staring at the plastic bag when the room outside vanished.

For a long time there was nothing at all. Nothing beyond the crystal mesh of the cage. Thoughts rushed through Conger's mind, helter-skelter. How would he know the man? How could he be certain, in advance? What had he looked like? What was his name? How had he acted, before he spoke? Would he be an ordinary person, or some strange outlandish crank?

Conger picked up the Slem-gun and held it against his cheek. The metal of the gun was cool and smooth. He practiced moving the sight. It was a beautiful gun, the kind of gun he could fall in love with. If he had owned such a gun in the Martian desert—on the long nights when he had lain, cramped and numbed with cold, waiting for things that moved through the darkness—

He put the gun down and adjusted the meter readings of the cage. The spiraling mist was beginning to condense and settle. All at once forms wavered and fluttered around him.

Colors, sounds, movements filtered through the crystal wire. He clamped the controls off and stood up.

HE WAS ON A RIDGE OVERLOOKING A small town. It was high noon. The air was crisp and bright. A few automobiles moved along a road. Off in the distance were some level fields. Conger went to the door and stepped outside. He sniffed the air. Then he went back into the cage.

He stood before the mirror over the shelf, examining his features. He had trimmed his beard—they had not got him to cut it off—and his hair was neat. He was dressed in the clothing of the middle-twentieth century, the odd collar and coat, the shoes of animal hide. In his pocket was money of the times. That was important. Nothing more was needed.

Nothing, except his ability, his special cunning. But he had never used it in such a way before.

He walked down the road toward the town.

The first things he noticed were the newspapers on the stands. April 5, 1961. He was not too far off. He looked around him. There was a filling station, a garage, some taverns, and a ten-cent store. Down the street was a grocery store and some public buildings.

A few minutes later he mounted the stairs of the little public library and passed through the doors into the warm interior.

The librarian looked up, smiling. "Good afternoon," she said.

He smiled, not speaking because his words would not be correct; accented and strange, probably. He went over to a table and sat down by a heap of magazines. For a moment he glanced through them. Then he was on his feet again. He crossed the room to a wide rack against the wall. His heart began to beat heavily.

Newspapers—weeks on end. He took a roll of them over to the table and began to scan them quickly. The print was odd, the letters strange. Some of the words were unfamiliar.

He set the papers aside and searched farther. At last he found what he wanted. He carried the *Cherrywood Gazette* to the table and opened it to the first page. He found what he wanted:

PRISONER HANGS SELF

An unidentified man, held by the county sheriff's office for suspicion of criminal syndicalism, was found dead this morning, by—

He finished the item. It was vague, uninforming. He needed more. He carried the *Gazette* back to the racks and then, after a moment's hesitation, approached the librarian.

"More?" he asked. "More papers. Old ones?"

She frowned. "How old? Which papers?"

"Months old. And—before."

"Of the *Gazette*? This is all we have. What did you want? What are you looking for? Maybe I can help you."

He was silent.

"You might find older issues at the *Gazette* office," the woman said, taking off her glasses. "Why don't you try there? But if you'd tell me, maybe I could help you—»

He went out.

The *Gazette* office was down a side street; the sidewalk was broken and cracked. He went inside. A heater glowed in the corner of the small office. A heavy-set man stood up and came slowly over to the counter.

"What did you want, mister?" he said.

"Old papers. A month. Or more."

"To buy? You want to buy them?"

"Yes." He held out some of the money he had. The man stared.

"Sure," he said. "Sure. Wait a minute." He went quickly out of the room. When he came back he was staggering under the weight of his armload, his face red. "Here are some," he grunted. "Took what I could find. Covers the whole year. And if you want more—»

Conger carried the papers outside. He sat down by the road and began to go through them.

WHAT HE WANTED WAS FOUR MONTHS back, in December. It was a tiny item, so small that he almost missed it. His hands trembled as he scanned it, using the small dictionary for some of the archaic terms.

MAN ARRESTED
FOR UNLICENSED
DEMONSTRATION

An unidentified man who refused to give his name was picked up in Cooper Creek by special agents of the sheriff's office, according to Sheriff Duff. It was said the man was recently noticed in this area and had been watched continually. It was—

Cooper Creek. December, 1960. His heart pounded. That was all he needed to know. He stood up, shaking himself, stamping his feet on the cold ground. The sun had moved across the sky to the very edge of the hills. He smiled. Already he had discovered the exact time and place. Now he needed only to go back, perhaps to November, to Cooper Creek—

He walked back through the main section of town, past the library, past the grocery store. It would not be hard; the hard part was over. He would go there; rent a room, prepare to wait until the man appeared.

He turned the corner. A woman was coming out of a doorway, loaded down with packages. Conger stepped aside to let her pass. The woman glanced at him. Suddenly her face turned white. She stared, her mouth open.

Conger hurried on. He looked back. What was wrong with her? The woman was still staring; she had dropped the packages to the ground. He increased his speed. He turned a second corner and went up a side street. When he looked back again the woman had come to the entrance of the street and was starting after him. A man joined her, and the two of them began to run toward him.

He lost them and left the town, striding quickly, easily, up into the hills at the edge of town. When he reached the cage he stopped. What had happened? Was it something about his clothing? His dress?

He pondered. Then, as the sun set, he stepped into the cage.

Conger sat before the wheel. For a moment he waited, his hands resting lightly on the control. Then he turned the wheel, just a little, following the control readings carefully.

The grayness settled down around him.

But not for very long.

THE MAN LOOKED HIM OVER CRITI-cally. "You better come inside," he said. "Out of the cold."

"Thanks." Conger went grate-fully through the open door, into the living-room. It was warm and close from the heat of the little kerosene heater in the corner. A woman, large and shape-less in her flowered dress, came from the kitchen. She and the man studied him critically.

"It's a good room," the woman said. "I'm Mrs. Appleton. It's got heat. You need that this time of year."

"Yes." He nodded, looking around.

"You want to eat with us?"

"What?"

"You want to eat with us?" The man's brows knitted. "You're not a for-eigner, are you, mister?"

"No." He smiled. "I was born in this country. Quite far west, though."

"California?"

"No." He hesitated. "In Oregon."

"What's it like up there?" Mrs. Appleton asked. "I hear there's a lot of trees and green. It's so barren here. I come from Chicago, myself."

"That's the Middle West," the man said to her. "You ain't no foreigner."

"Oregon isn't foreign, either," Con-ger said. "It's part of the United States."

The man nodded absently. He was staring at Conger's clothing.

"That's a funny suit you got on, mister," he said. "Where'd you get that?"

Conger was lost. He shifted uneas-ily. "It's a good suit," he said. "Maybe I better go some other place, if you don't want me here."

They both raised their hands pro-testingly. The woman smiled at him. "We just have to look out for those Reds. You know, the government is always warning us about them."

"The Reds?" He was puzzled.

"The government says they're all around. We're supposed to report any-thing strange or unusual, anybody doesn't act normal."

„Like me?"

They looked embarrassed. "Well, you don't look like a Red to me," the man said. "But we have to be careful. The *Tribune* says—»

Conger half listened. It was going to be easier than he had thought. Clearly, he would know as soon as the Founder appeared. These people, so suspicious of anything different, would be buzzing and gossiping and spreading the story. All he had to do was lie low and listen, down at the general store, perhaps. Or even here, in Mrs. Appleton's boarding house.

"Can I see the room?" he said.

"Certainly." Mrs. Appleton went to the stairs. "I'll be glad to show it to you."

They went upstairs. It was colder upstairs, but not nearly as cold as out-side. Nor as cold as nights on the Mar-tian deserts. For that he was grateful.

*   *   *

HE WAS WALKING SLOWLY AROUND the store, looking at the cans of vegetables, the frozen packages of fish and meats shining and clean in the open refrigerator counters.

Ed Davies came toward him. "Can I help you?" he said. The man was a little oddly dressed, and with a beard! Ed couldn't help smiling.

"Nothing," the man said in a funny voice. "Just looking."

"Sure," Ed said. He walked back behind the counter. Mrs. Hacket was wheeling her cart up.

"Who's he?" she whispered, her sharp face turned, her nose moving, as if it were sniffing. "I never seen him before."

"I don't know."

"Looks funny to me. Why does he wear a beard? No one else wears a beard. Must be something the matter with him."

"Maybe he likes to wear a beard. I had an uncle who—»

"Wait." Mrs. Hacket stiffened. "Didn't that—what was his name? The Red—that old one. Didn't he have a beard? Marx. He had a beard."

Ed laughed. "This ain't Karl Marx. I saw a photograph of him once."

Mrs. Hacket was staring at him. "You did?"

"Sure." He flushed a little. "What's the matter with that?"

"I'd sure like to know more about him," Mrs. Hacket said. "I think we ought to know more, for our own good."

*   *   *

"HEY, MISTER! WANT A RIDE?"

Conger turned quickly, dropping his hand to his belt. He relaxed. Two young kids in a car, a girl and a boy. He smiled at them. "A ride? Sure."

Conger got into the car and closed the door. Bill Willet pushed the gas and the car roared down the highway.

"I appreciate a ride," Conger said carefully. "I was taking a walk between towns, but it was farther than I thought."

"Where are you from?" Lora Hunt asked. She was pretty, small and dark, in her yellow sweater and blue skirt.

"From Cooper Creek."

"Cooper Creek?" Bill said. He frowned. "That's funny. I don't remember seeing you before."

"Why, do you come from there?"

"I was born there. I know everybody there."

"I just moved in. From Oregon."

"From Oregon? I didn't know Oregon people had accents."

"Do I have an accent?"

"You use words funny."

"How?"

"I don't know. Doesn't he, Lora?"

"You slur them," Lora said, smiling. "Talk some more. I'm interested in dialects." She glanced at him, white-teethed. Conger felt his heart constrict.

"I have a speech impediment."

"Oh." Her eyes widened. "I'm sorry."

They looked at him curiously as the car purred along. Conger for his part was struggling to find some way of asking them questions without seeming curious. "I guess people from out of town don't come here much," he said. "Strangers."

"No." Bill shook his head. "Not very much."

"I'll bet I'm the first outsider for a long time."

"I guess so."

Conger hesitated. "A friend of mine—someone I know, might be coming through here. Where do you suppose I might—" He stopped. "Would there be anyone certain to see him? Someone I could ask, make sure I don't miss him if he comes?"

They were puzzled. "Just keep your eyes open. Cooper Creek isn't very big."

"No. That's right."

They drove in silence. Conger studied the outline of the girl. Probably she was the boy's mistress. Perhaps she was his trial wife. Or had they developed trial marriage back so far? He could not remember. But surely such an attractive girl would be someone's mistress by this time; she would be sixteen or so, by her looks. He might ask her sometime, if they ever met again.

THE NEXT DAY CONGER WENT WALKING along the one main street of Cooper Creek. He passed the general store, the two filling stations, and then the post office. At the corner was the soda fountain.

He stopped. Lora was sitting inside, talking to the clerk. She was laughing, rocking back and forth.

Conger pushed the door open. Warm air rushed around him. Lora was drinking hot chocolate, with whipped cream. She looked up in surprise as he slid into the seat beside her.

"I beg your pardon," he said. "Am I intruding?"

"No." She shook her head. Her eyes were large and dark. "Not at all."

The clerk came over. "What do you want?"

Conger looked at the chocolate. "Same as she has."

Lora was watching Conger, her arms folded, elbows on the counter. She smiled at him. "By the way. You don't know my name. Lora Hunt."

She was holding out her hand. He took it awkwardly, not knowing what to do with it. "Conger is my name," he murmured.

"Conger? Is that your last or first name?"

"Last or first?" He hesitated. "Last. Omar Conger."

"Omar?" She laughed. "That's like the poet, Omar Khayyam."

"I don't know of him. I know very little of poets. We restored very few works of art. Usually only the Church has been interested enough—" He broke off. She was staring. He flushed. "Where I come from," he finished.

"The Church? Which church do you mean?"

"The Church." He was confused. The chocolate came and he began to sip it gratefully. Lora was still watching him.

"You're an unusual person," she said. "Bill didn't like you, but he never likes anything different. He's so—so prosaic. Don't you think that when a person gets older he should become—broadened in his outlook?"

Conger nodded.

"He says foreign people ought to stay where they belong, not come here. But you're not so foreign. He means orientals; you know."

Conger nodded.

The screen door opened behind them. Bill came into the room. He stared at them. "Well," he said.

Conger turned. "Hello."

"Well." Bill sat down. "Hello, Lora." He was looking at Conger. "I didn't expect to see you here."

Conger tensed. He could feel the hostility of the boy. "Something wrong with that?"

"No. Nothing wrong with it."

There was silence. Suddenly Bill turned to Lora. "Come on. Let's go."

"Go?" She was astonished. "Why?"

"Just go!" He grabbed her hand. "Come on! The car's outside."

"Why, Bill Willet," Lora said. "You're jealous!"

"Who is this guy?" Bill said. "Do you know anything about him? Look at him, his beard—»

She flared. "So what? Just because he doesn't drive a Packard and go to Cooper High!"

Conger sized the boy up. He was big—big and strong. Probably he was part of some civil control organization.

"Sorry," Conger said. "I'll go."

"What's your business in town?" Bill asked. "What are you doing here? Why are you hanging around Lora?"

Conger looked at the girl. He shrugged. "No reason. I'll see you later."

He turned away. And froze. Bill had moved. Conger's fingers went to his belt. *Half pressure*, he whispered to himself. *No more. Half pressure.*

He squeezed. The room leaped around him. He himself was protected by the lining of his clothing, the plastic sheathing inside.

"My God—" Lora put her hands up. Conger cursed. He hadn't meant any of it for her. But it would wear off. There was only a half-amp to it. It would tingle.

Tingle, and paralyze.

He walked out the door without looking back. He was almost to the corner when Bill came slowly out, holding onto the wall like a drunken man. Conger went on.

★ ★ ★

As Conger walked, restless, in the night, a form loomed in front of him. He stopped, holding his breath.

"Who is it?" a man's voice came. Conger waited, tense.

"Who is it?" the man said again. He clicked something in his hand. A light flashed. Conger moved.

"It's me," he said.

"Who is 'me'?"

"Conger is my name. I'm staying at the Appleton's place. Who are you?"

The man came slowly up to him. He was wearing a leather jacket. There was a gun at his waist.

"I'm Sheriff Duff. I think you're the person I want to talk to. You were in Bloom's today, about three o'clock?"

"Bloom's?"

"The fountain. Where the kids hang out." Duff came up beside him, shining his light into Conger's face. Conger blinked.

"Turn that thing away," he said.

A pause. "All right." The light flickered to the ground. "You were there. Some trouble broke out between you and the Willet boy. Is that right? You had a beef over his girl—»

"We had a discussion," Conger said carefully.

"Then what happened?"

"Why?"

"I'm just curious. They say you did something."

"Did something? Did what?"

"I don't know. That's what I'm wondering. They saw a flash, and something seemed to happen. They all blacked out. Couldn't move."

"How are they now?"

"All right."

There was silence.

"Well?" Duff said. "What was it? A bomb?"

"A bomb?" Conger laughed. "No. My cigarette lighter caught fire. There was a leak, and the fluid ignited."

"Why did they all pass out?"

"Fumes."

Silence. Conger shifted, waiting. His fingers moved slowly toward his belt. The Sheriff glanced down. He grunted.

"If you say so," he said. "Anyhow, there wasn't any real harm done." He stepped back from Conger. "And that Willet is a trouble-maker."

"Good night, then," Conger said. He started past the Sheriff.

"One more thing, Mr. Conger. Before you go. You don't mind if I look at your identification, do you?"

"No. Not at all." Conger reached into his pocket. He held his wallet out. The Sheriff took it and shined his flashlight on it. Conger watched, breathing shallowly. They had worked hard on the wallet, studying historic documents, relics of the times, all the papers they felt would be relevant.

Duff handed it back. "Okay. Sorry to bother you." The light winked off.

When Conger reached the house he found the Appletons sitting around the television set. They did not look up as he came in. He lingered at the door.

"Can I ask you something?" he said. Mrs. Appleton turned slowly. "Can I ask you—what's the date?"

"The date?" She studied him. "The first of December."

"December first! Why, it was just November!"

They were all looking at him. Suddenly he remembered. In the twentieth century they still used the old twelve-month system. November fed directly into December; there was no Quartember between.

He gasped. Then it was tomorrow! The second of December! Tomorrow!

"Thanks," he said. "Thanks."

He went up the stairs. What a fool he was, forgetting. The Founder had been taken into captivity on the second of December, according to the newspaper records. Tomorrow, only twelve hours hence, the Founder would appear to speak to the people and then be dragged away.

THE DAY WAS WARM AND BRIGHT. Conger's shoes crunched the melting crust of snow. On he went, through the trees heavy with white. He climbed a hill and strode down the other side, sliding as he went.

He stopped to look around. Everything was silent. There was no one in sight. He brought a thin rod from his waist and turned the handle of it. For a moment nothing happened. Then there was a shimmering in the air.

The crystal cage appeared and settled slowly down. Conger sighed. It was good to see it again. After all, it was his only way back.

He walked up on the ridge. He looked around with some satisfaction, his hands on his hips. Hudson's field was spread out, all the way to the beginning of town. It was bare and flat, covered with a thin layer of snow.

Here, the Founder would come. Here, he would speak to them. And here the authorities would take him.

Only he would be dead before they came. He would be dead before he even spoke.

Conger returned to the crystal globe. He pushed through the door and stepped inside. He took the Slem-gun from the shelf and screwed the bolt into place. It was ready to go, ready to fire. For a moment he considered. Should he have it with him?

No. It might be hours before the Founder came, and suppose someone approached him in the meantime? When he saw the Founder coming toward the field, then he could go and get the gun.

Conger looked toward the shelf. There was the neat plastic package. He took it down and unwrapped it.

He held the skull in his hands, turning it over. In spite of himself, a cold feeling rushed through him. This was the man's skull, the skull of the Founder, who was still alive, who would come here, this day, who would stand on the field not fifty yards away.

What if *he* could see this, his own skull, yellow and eroded? Two centuries old. Would he still speak? Would he speak, if he could see it, the grinning, aged skull? What would there be for him to say, to tell the people? What message could he bring?

What action would not be futile, when a man could look upon his own aged, yellowed skull? Better they should enjoy their temporary lives, while they still had them to enjoy.

A man who could hold his own skull in his hands would believe in few causes, few movements. Rather, he would preach the opposite—

A sound. Conger dropped the skull back on the shelf and took up the gun. Outside something was moving. He went quickly to the door, his heart beating. Was it *he*? Was it the Founder, wandering by himself in the cold, looking for a place to speak? Was he meditating over his words, choosing his sentences?

What if he could see what Conger had held!

He pushed the door open, the gun raised.

Lora!

He stared at her. She was dressed in a wool jacket and boots, her hands in her pockets. A cloud of steam came from her mouth and nostrils. Her breast was rising and falling.

Silently, they looked at each other. At last Conger lowered the gun.

"What is it?" he said. "What are you doing here?"

She pointed. She did not seem able to speak. He frowned; what was wrong with her?

"What is it?" he said. "What do you want?" He looked in the direction she had pointed. "I don't see anything."

"They're coming."

"They? Who? Who are coming?"

"They are. The police. During the night the Sheriff had the state police send cars. All around, everywhere. Blocking the roads. There's about sixty of them coming. Some from town, some around behind." She stopped, gasping. "They said—they said—»

"What?"

"They said you were some kind of a Communist. They said—»

CONGER WENT INTO THE CAGE. He put the gun down on the shelf and came back out. He leaped down and went to the girl.

"Thanks. You came here to tell me? You don't believe it?"

"I don't know."

"Did you come alone?"

"No. Joe brought me in his truck. From town."

"Joe? Who's he?"

"Joe French. The plumber. He's a friend of Dad's."

"Let's go." They crossed the snow, up the ridge and onto the field. The little panel truck was parked half way across the field. A heavy short man was sitting behind the wheel, smoking his pipe. He sat up as he saw the two of them coming toward him.

"Are you the one?" he said to Conger.

"Yes. Thanks for warning me."

The plumber shrugged. "I don't know anything about this. Lora says you're all right." He turned around. "It might interest you to know some more of them are coming. Not to warn you—just curious."

"More of them?" Conger looked toward the town. Black shapes were picking their way across the snow.

"People from the town. You can't keep this sort of thing quiet, not in a small town. We all listen to the police radio; they heard the same way Lora did. Someone tuned in, spread it around—»

The shapes were getting closer. Conger could, make out a couple of them. Bill Willet was there, with some boys from the high school. The Appletons were along, hanging back in the rear.

"Even Ed Davies," Conger murmured.

The storekeeper was toiling onto the field, with three or four other men from the town.

"All curious as hell," French said. "Well, I guess I'm going back to town. I don't want my truck shot full of holes. Come on, Lora."

She was looking up at Conger, wide-eyed.

"Come on," French said again. "Let's go. You sure as hell can't stay here, you know."

"Why?"

"There may be shooting. That's what they all came to see. You know that don't you, Conger?"

"Yes."

"You have a gun? Or don't you care?" French smiled a little. "They've picked up a lot of people in their time, you know. You won't be lonely."

He cared, all right! He had to stay here, on the field. He couldn't afford to let them take him away. Any minute the Founder would appear, would step onto the field. Would he be one of the townsmen, standing silently at the foot of the field, waiting, watching?

Or maybe he was Joe French. Or maybe one of the cops. Anyone of them might find himself moved to speak. And the few words spoken this day were going to be important for a long time.

And Conger had to be there, ready when the first word was uttered!

"I care," he said. "You go on back to town. Take the girl with you."

Lora got stiffly in beside Joe French. The plumber started up the motor. "Look at them, standing there," he said. "Like vultures. Waiting to see someone get killed."

THE TRUCK DROVE AWAY, LORA sitting stiff and silent, frightened now. Conger watched for a moment. Then he dashed back into the woods, between the trees, toward the ridge.

He could get away, of course. Anytime he wanted to he could get away. All he had to do was to leap into the crystal cage and turn the handles. But he had a job, an important job. He had to be here, here at this place, at this time.

He reached the cage and opened the door. He went inside and picked up the gun from the shelf. The Slem-gun would take care of them. He notched it up to full count. The chain reaction from it would flatten them all, the police, the curious, sadistic people—

They wouldn't take him! Before they got him, all of them would be dead. *He* would get away. He would escape. By the end of the day they would all be dead, if that was what they wanted, and he—

He saw the skull.

Suddenly he put the gun down. He picked up the skull. He turned the skull over. He looked at the teeth. Then he went to the mirror.

He held the skull up, looking in the mirror. He pressed the skull against his cheek. Beside his own face the grinning skull leered back at him, beside *his* skull, against his living flesh.

He bared his teeth. And he knew.

It was his own skull that he held. He was the one who would die. He was the Founder.

After a time he put the skull down. For a few minutes he stood at the controls, playing with them idly. He could hear the sound of motors outside, the muffled noise of men. Should he go back to the present, where the Speaker waited? He could escape, of course—

Escape?

He turned toward the skull. There it was, his skull, yellow with age. Escape? Escape, when he had held it in his own hands?

What did it matter if he put it off a month, a year, ten years, even fifty? Time was nothing. He had sipped chocolate with a girl born a hundred and fifty years before his time. Escape? For a little while, perhaps.

But he could not *really* escape, no more so than anyone else had ever escaped, or ever would.

Only, he had held it in his hands, his own bones, his own death's-head.

They had not.

He went out the door and across the field, empty handed. There were a lot of them standing around, gathered together, waiting. They expected a good fight; they knew he had something. They had heard about the incident at the fountain.

And there were plenty of police—police with guns and tear gas, creeping across the hills and ridges, between the trees, closer and closer. It was an old story, in this century.

One of the men tossed something at him. It fell in the snow by his feet, and he looked down. It was a rock. He smiled.

"Come on!" one of them called. "Don't you have any bombs?"

"Throw a bomb! You with the beard! Throw a bomb!"

"Let 'em have it!"

"Toss a few A Bombs!"

★ ★ ★

THEY BEGAN TO LAUGH. HE SMILED. He put his hands to his hips. They suddenly turned silent, seeing that he was going to speak.

"I'm sorry," he said simply. "I don't have any bombs. You're mistaken."

There was a flurry of murmuring.

"I have a gun," he went on. "A very good one. Made by science even more advanced than your own. But I'm not going to use that, either."

They were puzzled.

"Why not?" someone called. At the edge of the group an older woman was watching. He felt a sudden shock. He had seen her before. Where?

He remembered. The day at the library. As he had turned the corner he had seen her. She had noticed him and been astounded. At the time, he did not understand why.

Conger grinned. So he *would* escape death, the man who right now was voluntarily accepting it. They were laughing, laughing at a man who had a gun but didn't use it. But by a strange twist of science he would appear again, a few months later, after his bones had been buried under the floor of a jail.

And so, in a fashion, he would escape death. He would die, but then, after a period of months, he would live again, briefly, for an afternoon.

An afternoon. Yet long enough for them to see him, to understand that he was still alive. To know that somehow he had returned to life.

And then, finally, he would appear once more, after two hundred years had passed. Two centuries later.

He would be born again, born, as a matter of fact, in a small trading village on Mars. He would grow up, learning to hunt and trade—

A police car came on the edge of the field and stopped. The people retreated a little. Conger raised his hands.

"I have an odd paradox for you," he said. "Those who take lives will lose their own. Those who kill, will die. But he who gives his own life away will live again!"

They laughed, faintly, nervously. The police were coming out, walking toward him. He smiled. He had said everything he intended to say. It was a good little paradox he had coined. They would puzzle over it, remember it.

Smiling, Conger awaited a death foreordained.

THE END

CONTRIBUTORS

MICHAEL BUNKER is a *USA Today* Bestselling author, off-gridder, husband, and father of four children. He lives with his family in Central Texas where he reads and writes books…and occasionally tilts at windmills. In November of 2015, Variety Magazine announced that Michael had sold a film/tv option for his bestselling novel *Pennsylvania* to Jorgensen Pictures.

PHILIP K. DICK (1928 – 1982), was an American science fiction writer and novelist. He wrote 44 novels and about 121 short stories, most of which appeared in science fiction magazines during his lifetime.

ROBERT FROST (1874 – 1963) was an American poet known for his realistic depictions of rural life and his command of American colloquial speech.

NATHANIEL HAWTHORNE (1804 – 1864) was an American novelist and short story writer. His works often focus on history, morality, and religion.

ALISTIAR FOLEY is a creative writing teacher that teaches at the Northern Virginia Community College in Carmel, Virginia. He enjoys mainstream fantasy novels and long walks on the beach. He lives alone with his cats, Frodo, Samwise, Merry, Pippin, Aragorn, Legolas, Gimli, Boromir and Fluffy.

HERMAN MELVILLE (1819 – 1891) was an American novelist, short story writer, and poet of the American Renaissance period. Among his best-known works are *Moby-Dick, Typee,* and *Billy Budd, Sailor*. At the time of his death, Melville was no longer well known to the public, but the 1919 centennial of his birth was the starting point of a Melville revival. *Moby-Dick* eventually would be considered one of the great American novels.

KEVIN G. SUMMERS is the author of *Legendarium, The Man Who Shot John Wilkes Booth*, and *The Bleak December*.

BOOTH TARKINGTON (1869 – 1946) was an American novelist and dramatist best known for his novels The Magnificent Ambersons (1918) and Alice Adams (1921). He is one of only four novelists to win the Pulitzer Prize for Fiction more than once.

STUART WILLIAMS (1946 – 2004) was a Scottish-Canadian writer and editor of American horror-comics magazines, best known for his work with the 1970s publisher Skywald Publications, where he created what he termed the magazines' "Horror-Mood" sensibility.

BACKISSUE BULLETIN! • BACKISSUE BULLETIN! • BACKISSUE BULLETIN!

AN ADVENTURE

ON EVERY PAGE!

BACK ISSUES ARE STILL AVAILABLE! If you missed out on any of our first four issues we have a limited amount in stock at Wonder City eBay store. Just log on to eBay and type in the word Collectorzine!

Every issue features an exclusive Chakan the Forever Man story by Indy Comics legend Robert "RAK" Kraus. And you won't want to miss out on the two part Mike W. Barr interview in issues one and two. Each issue features original stories, reviews, and tips to help you get the most out of reading and collecting comics.

WE ARE ACCEPTING SUBMISSIONS! For more information about appearing in *Collectorzine Magazine*, contact us at: collectorzine@gmail.com. We would like to see you in future issues of our fantabulous fanzine!

We don't want to sell you just a comic book. We want to sell you a collectible!

www.ingramcontent.com/pod-product-compliance
Lightning Source LLC
Chambersburg PA
CBHW080841160726
47999CB00009B/2967